Free To Be... A Family

Conceived by
Marlo Thomas

Executive Editor: Marlo Thomas
Editor: Christopher Cerf
Consulting Editor: Letty Cottin Pogrebin
Contributing Editors: Carol Hall, Sarah Durkee,
Wendy Goldwyn, Norman Stiles
Director of Art and Design: Barbara N. Cohen

BANTAM BOOKS
TORONTO · NEW YORK · LONDON · SYDNEY · AUCKLAND

Advisors

James P. Comer, M.D., Maurice Falk Professor of Child Psychiatry,
Yale University Child Study Center

Maureen Crossmaker, Project Director for Assault Prevention Training,
National Assault Prevention Center

Merle Froschl, Founder and Co-Coordinator, Women and Disability Awareness Project,
and Co-Director, Educational Equity Concepts, Inc.

Ellen Galinsky, Director of Work and Family Life Studies,
Bank Street College of Education

Margaret Gates, National Executive Director, Girls Clubs of America

Phyllis Katz, Ph.D., Director, Institute for Research on Social Problems

James Levine, Director, The Fatherhood Project,
Bank Street College of Education

Joseph Pleck, Ph.D., Henry R. Luce Professor of Families, Change and Society,
Wheaton College

Special Thanks

To Eddie Adams, David Allender, Stuart Applebaum, Joanne Barkan, Karen Barnes, Karin Berg, Kathie Berlin, Marc Black, Dawn Bridges, David Britt, Sue Brownlees, Patricia T. Carbine, Seymour Chwast, Judie Clarke, Sally Cooper, Jean Enderson, Phyllis Flood, Michael Frith, Nancy Gallt, Angelina Genduso, Darcy Gilpin, Mary Rodgers Guettel, Jay Harnick, Andrew Helfer, Jim Henson, Jackson Typesetters, Rudy Jordan, Jenette Kahn, Lisa Kennedy, Fern Khan, John Knapp, Danica Kombol, W. A. Krueger Co., Gary Lapow, Sharon Lerner, Robert F. Levine, Paul Levitz, Vinnie Liguori, Marilu Lopez, Sonia Manzano, Barry Marx, Maxwell Photographics, Inc., Dr. David Milrod, Kathryn Mullen, Manuel and Kate Neri, Mary Phylis, Jim Plumeri, Ann Poe, Jill Rabon, Nancy Rose, Lili Rosenstreich, Stephen Rubin, Richard Ruopp, Donna Ruvituso, Heidi Sachner, Lucy Salvino, Ray Sander, Nancy Sans, Herb Sargent, Kathryn Schenker, Jeff Segal, Virginia Solotaroff, Judy Stagnitto, Katie Swanson, Tani Takagi, Iwao Takamoto, Eric Taylor, Lily Tomlin, Rusty Unger, Jerry White, Vernon White, Marie Wilson, Perla Winer, Harriet Yassky, Jaye Zimet, to the Children, Parents, Teachers, and Staff of P.S. 146 in Manhattan and the Bank Street School and
especially to Elizabeth Anne Perle.

Musical arrangements for this book by Paul Jacobs

FREE TO BE...A FAMILY

A Bantam Book / November 1987

Grateful acknowledgment is made for permission to publish the following:
"A Father Like That," Text copyright © 1971 by Charlotte Zolotow. Reprinted by permission of Harper & Row Publishers, Inc.; "I'll Fix Anthony," Text copyright © 1969 by Judith Viorst. Illustrations copyright © 1969 by Arnold Lobel. Reprinted by permission of Harper & Row Publishers, Inc.; "Stevie," Copyright © 1969 by John L. Steptoe. Reprinted by permission of Harper & Row Publishers, Inc.; "Crowded Tub," Copyright © 1981 by Evil Eye Music, Inc.; "The Little Boy and the Old Man," Copyright © 1981 by Evil Eye Music, Inc.; "And Superboy Makes 3," SUPERBOY, SUPERMAN and all other characters in "And Superboy Makes 3," their distinctive likenesses and related indicia, are trademarks of DC Comics Inc. Copyright © 1987 by DC Comics Inc. Published under license.; "Some Things Don't Make Any Sense at All," Text copyright © 1981 by Judith Viorst. Reprinted by permission of Atheneum Publishers, Inc.; "On My Pond," Text copyright © 1987 by Splotched Animal Music and Jive Durkee Music. KERMIT THE FROG is a trademark of Henson Associates, Inc. Illustrations copyright © 1987 by Henson Associates, Inc. "On My Pond," is adapted from a SESAME STREET sequence. SESAME STREET is a trademark and service mark of Children's Television Workshop.; "From Here to Forever," Copyright ©, 1984, 1987 by Music City Music, Inc. (ASCAP) and Resaca Music Publishing Company (BMI).; "Lily Tomlin's Edith Ann in And That's the Truth," Copyright © 1987 by Lily Tomlin and Jane Wagner.; "All Us Come Cross the Water," Text copyright © 1973 by Lucille Clifton. Illustrations copyright © 1973 by John L. Steptoe. "All Us Come Cross the Water" has been adapted for use in this publication. Originally published by Holt, Rinehart and Winston; "Little Abigail and the Beautiful Pony," Copyright © 1981 by Evil Eye Music, Inc.; "Like Me," by Emily Kingsley was suggested by JUST LIKE ME, a book by Jennifer Fink. Photos for The Fat Boys collage courtesy of Eddie Adams, Steve Friedman, Paul Natkin and Tin Pan Apple. Photo for "Twanna and Me," copyright © 1987 Jonathan Becker. "Boy Meets Girl Plus One" by Peter Stone is based upon "Boy Meets Girl" by Peter Stone and Carl Reiner.

Library of Congress Cataloging-in-Publication Data

Free to be—a family.

Summary: A collection of stories, poems and songs about different types of families and family relationships.
1. Family life—Literary collections.   2. Children's literature. [1. Family life—Literary collections.
2. Short stories.   3. American poetry—Collections.
4. Songs]   I. Thomas, Marlo.
PZ5.F855   1987   [FIC]   87-47581
ISBN 0-553-05235-7

Published simultaneously in the United States and Canada

Contents

6   Foreword *by Marlo Thomas*

8   A Note to Parents, Teachers and Other
     Grown-Up Friends *by Letty Cottin Pogrebin*

10   What Buying This Book Will Do
     by Gloria Steinem

12   Free To Be…A Family
     by Sarah Durkee and Paul Jacobs

14   Boy Meets Girl Plus One *by Peter Stone*

20   A Tale of Three Ralphs
     by Miriam Minkowitz

23   Friendly Neighborhood
     by Lynn Ahrens and Stephen Flaherty

25   Another Cinderella *by Norman Stiles*

33   Little Abigail and the Beautiful Pony
     by Shel Silverstein

34   Some Things Don't Make Any Sense at All
     by Judith Viorst

35   Stevie *by John Steptoe*

38   I'll Fix Anthony *by Judith Viorst*

42   It's Not My Fault
     by Sarah Durkee and Christopher Cerf

44   The Right Family *by Sarah Durkee*

49   Crowded Tub *by Shel Silverstein*

50   In My Room *by Bobby Gosh*

52   My Grandma *by Letty Cottin Pogrebin*

57   And Superboy Makes 3
     by Mark Saltzman, Edited by Joe Orlando

65   The Entertainer *by Jeff Moss*

68   I'm Never Afraid
     (To Say What's on My Mind)
     by Sarah Durkee and Christopher Cerf

70   Letters From Camp *by Sarah Durkee*

74   Two Can Play the Same Game
     by Mavis Jukes

78   A Father Like That *by Charlotte Zolotow*

83   The Day Dad Made Toast *by Sarah Durkee*

90   The Stupid Song *by Robin Batteau*

92   Talk It Over
     by Carly Simon and Jacob Brackman

94   From Here to Forever
     *by Kris Kristofferson, Stephen Bruton,
     Glen Clark and Billy Swan*

96   The Night We Started Dancing
     by Ann Cameron

105 The Little Boy and the Old Man
     by Shel Silverstein

106 Twanna and Me *by Orlando Perez*

107 Like Me *by Emily Kingsley*

110 The Biggest Problem
     (Is in Other People's Minds)
     by Don Haynie

113 Cross Your Fingers *by Mavis Jukes*

122 Jimmy Says
     by David Buskin and Abra Bigham

124 Doris Knows Everything *by Whoopi Goldberg*

126 Yourself Belongs to You
     by The Fat Boys, with Jimmy Glenn

128 Lily Tomlin's Edith Ann in
     And That's the Truth
     by Jane Wagner

129 On My Pond *by Kermit the Frog,
     with Sarah Durkee and Christopher Cerf*

133 All Us Come Cross the Water
     by Lucille Clifton

138 Something for Everyone *by Carol Hall*

142 The Kingdom with No Rules, No Laws,
     and No King *by Norman Stiles*

148 The Turn of the Tide
     by Carly Simon and Jacob Brackman

150 We Need a Bigger Turkey
     by Norman Stiles and Christopher Cerf

153 We and They *by Lucille Clifton*

154 Thank Someone
     by Sarah Durkee and Paul Jacobs

156 Music for the Songs in
     Free To Be…A Family

172 Afterword *by Kurt Vonnegut, Jr.*

173 About the Contributors

Foreword

by Marlo Thomas

A few years ago when my niece Dionne was a little girl, she used to ask her grandfather (my daddy), "Grandpa, what's your job?"

And he answered, "My job is to be a comedian and an actor and make people laugh."

"So what's *my* job?" Dionne asked.

"Your job," he said, "is to learn how BIG the world is."

"How am I supposed to learn how BIG the world is when I'm so LITTLE?!" Dionne exclaimed.

"Start with your family," her grandfather answered. "Start with us."

Well, back then Dionne had a pretty small family. It was her and her mom and her dad. But since then, she's got a new little brother named Jason and three new girl cousins—Tracy, Kristina, and Kate—and since I've married in the meantime, she also has a new Uncle Phil and five new stepcousins from faraway cities like Chicago and Albuquerque, and she has a book called *Free To Be . . . You and Me,* which my friends and I created for her and which helped her learn how BIG her own life could be, how many different kinds of Dionnes she could become.

What I want her to have now is a GIGANTIC book, roomy enough to contain all the things she needs to know about this GIGANTIC variety of people who are clustered around her and calling themselves her family, calling themselves "us."

So my friends and I have written another book for my big niece Dionne and her little brother Jason and for Tracy, Kristina, and Kate, and for you, too. It's called *Free To Be . . . A Family*. It may look like a regular-sized book, but deep down inside, it's GIGANTIC. This book is like a balloon. The more you read it and use it, the more it stretches, the bigger it gets. There's room in it for all the kinds of families you can imagine, all the kinds of friends and relations we are to each other, all the different kinds of households we live in and love in.

Kids like you don't get to vote on how many grandmothers you have; maybe you'll have one, two, or four. The one you feel closest to may be the mother of the man your mom married after she and your dad were divorced. Or she may be the lady down the hall who stays with you until your mom comes home from work.

She may not really be your grandmother. But she sure *feels* like one, and that's what counts in a family.

Kids like you don't get to vote on who their brothers and sisters are. Maybe you'll have one brother and one sister and one dad and one mom forever and always; maybe you'll have one stepsister; maybe you'll have two blood sisters, one half-brother, and a Korean brother who was adopted. You may not have known him forever. But it sure *feels* like you have. And in a family, that's what counts.

If you start with the "us" in your life and study up on the folks in your family, chances are you'll be an expert on how to get along in the big, wide world when you grow up.

Dionne's five stepcousins and my stepchildren—Michael, Kevin, Dan, Jim, and Mary Rose—used to be jealous of other children who came from smaller families where nobody wore hand-me-downs or had to yell to get a word in edgewise at the dinner table.

Then they found out that other children were jealous of *them* because they had such a big family that there was always a bigger brother to dust you off and wipe your tears if you fell off your bike, there was always somebody around to fight with and play with.

Well, *Free To Be . . . A Family* is just too BIG for anything as small as being jealous of anybody.

Free To Be . . . A Family is full of songs and stories and jokes to help you and Dionne and all the cousins of all the cousins open your hearts to the possibilities that are already there in your very own "us." So, you'll know for sure how very lucky you are to have one grandmother or four grandmothers or a foster sister who speaks another language she can teach you or a half-brother who won't go to sleep until you read him a story from this book or, like Dionne's five stepcousins, a brand-new grandfather who is a comedian and an actor and makes all the people in our family laugh.

A Note to Parents, Teachers and Other Grown-Up Friends

by Letty Cottin Pogrebin

We're back. But why? Why, after all these years, have we decided to bring you *Free To Be, Part II*?

The answer is simple. We have new things to say and now is the time to say them.

Free To Be . . . You and Me was about becoming an authentic self, about children's autonomy and personal development.

Free To Be . . . A Family is about being together, about finding a balance between Self and Other, between privacy and attachment.

The first book was about independence. This book is about belonging . . . all kinds of belonging.

Now is the time to talk about all kinds of belonging because some people believe that there is only one kind. Many forces in our society recognize only one "legitimate" family structure and only one correct way of living together as a household. Society is always judging families to see if they conform to an ideal standard and making them feel bad if they don't. For instance, some people use words like "broken family" to describe a mom and her kids who don't feel at all in need of repair. And when some people say things like "The American family is in trouble," they don't mean we ought to be helping families get better housing or health care; they mean mothers ought to stay home and children ought to obey their elders.

Unfortunately, the people who say and think such things are often allowed to define family issues for the rest of us. But the majority of families do not conform to anyone's rigid model of "the right family," and the majority of families do not want other people telling them what their problem is.

Given how families have changed, we dedicate *Free To Be . . . A Family* to the "real" American family. *Yours.* We believe that whatever it looks like, wherever it lives, whomever it contains, each family is very real and precious to the people in it.

Just as our first book affirmed the true potential of the individual, this book celebrates the way American families really live today, and the truth is that they are marvelously adaptive and democratically diverse. In this country, adults and kids live in "traditional" families (about seven percent of households have a stay-home mother, an employed father, and their own biological children), two-paycheck families, stepfamilies, blended families, extended families, adoptive families, single-parent families, foster families, and others that have no label at all. We believe that labelled or not, each family is the "right" kind of family if it knows how to nourish, nurture, and love its children.

Since a child's family may be as vital to his or her basic identity as gender or color, it makes sense that *Free To Be . . . A Family* should challenge family stereotypes as a natural progression from *Free To Be . . . You and Me,* which challenged sex and racial stereotypes.

Kids cannot *choose* the family in which they are raised any more than they can choose to be born male or female, black or white, rich or poor. But how children *experience* each of these realities is determined by the way we adults evaluate our often unexamined assumptions about different personal attributes or family compositions. And just as children suffer from sexism and racism, they also hurt when their families are *discredited*—either directly or by inference or innuendo. Kids internalize societal criticism. They feel personally stigmatized. They blame themselves for not living "Dick and Jane" lives. They blame their parents for not being Mary Poppins or Doctor Dolittle.

In *Free To Be . . . A Family,* kids will find lots of terrific families but not one that is "perfect." (That's because there is no such thing.) Instead, they will find all kinds of families in all kinds of situations doing the best they can under the circumstances. Whether the circumstances are hilarious or fantastic or ordinary, kids will be able to identify with them.

In addition to humor, fantasy, and farce, this book also gives equal time to serious matters, to children's most touching moments and troubling realities: a parent's anger; adjusting to a new stepparent; the arrival of a new baby; the pain of sibling rivalry; fear of monsters and other terrible things; problems with peer pressure or with misguided attitudes about disability; worry about the beleaguered environment; mourning a loved one.

Happy or sad, silly or serious, each selection will either remind kids of their own families or expose them to other people's. They can compare problems and borrow solutions. They can get the "mad" out and laugh a lot and validate *all* their human connections—their family of origin, their extended family of relatives and friends, the cultural family of their ethnic group or community, and the global community to which we are all linked by human ecology, the nuclear threat, and a shared destiny.

In keeping with our theme, this book has a family, too. Our immediate family consists of Marlo Thomas and the many talented creators, writers, editors, entertainers, designers, and illustrators who shaped the enduring *Free To Be* vision to meet the needs of a new generation.

The book also has an extended family of experts and specialists who enthusiastically advised us and contributed to our research. Listed by name on page 4, they include noted educators and psychologists; activists working to end family violence; advocates for disability rights and for minority groups, poor families, adoptive parents and adopted children; and classrooms full of kids who brought us their honest feelings about their own family circumstances and life experiences.

Our extended family extends even further—to all the families who will benefit from the profits generated by the sale of this book. As with the first book, revenues from *Free To Be . . . A Family* go to the Ms. Foundation for Women and Children, which funds groups working to assure children's safety, health, and well-being: specifically, to increase the availability of child care and equal education and to prevent the tragedies of fetal alcohol syndrome, child abuse, incest, teen pregnancy, family poverty, hunger, and homelessness.

So this book has been a family project from start to finish. And now you and your family are joining our circle. Welcome! We know you'll feel right at home. We're pretty sure that somewhere in these pages you and your children or the children in your classes will each find your own story because this book tells the whole story—about all kinds of belonging.

What Buying This Book Will Do

by Gloria Steinem

I always thought my family was different from other families.

For one thing, we lived and traveled in a house trailer most of the winters before I was ten, so I learned to read and write from my parents and my older sister instead of going to school.

For another thing, my parents separated and divorced when I was about eleven. I don't remember feeling sad about that fact—I knew they both would be happier, and I knew they loved me no matter where we lived—but movies told me you were supposed to feel bad if your parents got divorced.

Finally, my very gentle and kind mother was sick a lot of the time, so I often cooked her meals and took care of her instead of the other way around.

All of this made me feel odd.

So, I envied my friend Linda who went to school like everybody else, and who lived with her mother and brother in a little apartment above a movie theater. How great to see your friends everyday, and to go downstairs to a movie whenever you wanted!

And I envied my friend Carol who lived in a neat little row house with her sister and brother and parents. How great to have your meals cooked for you and your clothes ironed for you, and to live in a house where you could invite your friends!

Most of all, I envied the kids in Hollywood movies who had fresh strawberries for breakfast, clean clothes every day, birthday parties, and even horses to ride.

Years later, I talked to my now grown-up friends and realized something very interesting. Linda said she had felt funny because her mother was a widow and they didn't live in a real house. Carol had been a little ashamed because her father went to work in overalls and didn't speak English very well. Both of them had envied me because I didn't have to go to school all the time, I had traveled to lots of different places, and I made up my own rules because I was being my own mother.

All of us felt a little bad because we didn't live the way that kids did in the movies.

Well, the first thing this book can do is show that movies and other made-up images aren't always right or real. Neither are all of our ideas about what a "real family" is. If we feel loved and supported for being special and unique, if we have enough food and a warm, dry place to live, if we have people we love and feel close to, then we are probably in a real family. It doesn't matter whether it is one we got born into, or one we chose, or one that chose us, or one that came together because people who already had families loved each other and decided to blend them into one.

Of course, there will always be problems, because problems are things that make us stronger tomorrow than we were today. That's how we grow. This book tells us that, too.

But no one way of living can be right for everybody. How boring the world would be if we were all alike! This book can help us feel good about ourselves and help us use our unique families to become the very best people we can be.

There *are* many children who don't feel loved and supported as the unique people they really are. There are many who don't have enough food or a safe place to live. There are some who are in real physical danger; sometimes from strangers and sometimes from the people in their very own house.

By buying this book, you are not only making yourself better and happier, you are also helping other children and families. All the writers and artists and editors and musicians who put it together cared so much about its subject that they decided to work for far less than their usual rates so that extra profits could go to the Free To Be Foundation and be given to very special multi-racial, non-sexist projects that help families and children to help themselves:

Projects that protect children from danger, and help children stay with the people they love.

Projects that make sure children's unique talents aren't limited because of race, or sex, or poverty, or anything else that we get born into.

Projects that help children stay healthy and grow up free.

If you would like to know more about these projects, just write for information to:

Free To Be Foundation
370 Lexington Avenue
New York, New York 10017

Marlo Thomas, Letty Cottin Pogrebin, and I are all on the Board, and we promise you that we will make every single dollar s-t-r-e-t-c-h to provide health and happiness and safety for children and families who need it.

We hope this book helps you. And we hope you like knowing that it helps others.

Free To Be . . . a Family

Words by Sarah Durkee, Music by Paul Jacobs
Illustrated by Susan Jeffers

♪ see page 156 for the music

We're all branches of the same big family tree,
but every family's different, don't you know?
Reachin' for the sun comes very naturally.
We've only got to let each other grow!

I've got a home . . .
I've found my place . . .
I live with people who are glad to see my face.

We're free to be . . .
you and me,
and you and me,
we're free to be . . . a family!

We're all workin' in the same big marching band,
but drums and horns have different things to say.
All together we'll ring music through the land
We've only got to let each other play!

I've got a place . . .
I've found my home . . .
I'm only solo when I want to be alone.

We're free to be . . .
you and me,
and you and me,
we're free to be . . . a family!

So many groups in the family soup,
So many combinations,
Might be people who look like you
or they might be no relation!
Birds of a feather, they flock together,
Yes, sometimes they do.
But if a little bird joins an elephant herd,
Hey, that's a family, too!

We're all cookin' up the same big barbeque,
but we like spicy, you like sticky sweet.
Maybe we can trade our recipe with you.
Then how about we help each other eat?!

This is my home . . .
These are my folks . . .
These are our secrets and our habits
    and our jokes.

We're free to be . . .
you and me,
and you and me,
we're free to be . . . a family!

Boy Meets Girl Plus One

by Peter Stone
Illustrated by Tom Cooke

The Place: A Park
The Time: One month later

BOY: Hi!

GIRL: Are you speaking to me?

BOY: I certainly am. Hi! Hi! Hi, there!

GIRL: Look, just because we're in the park and it's a beautiful day and I'm only a month old and I'm adorable, that doesn't give you the right to talk to strangers.

BOY: What strangers? Don't you remember me? The Hospital? Four weeks ago? That suave, debonaire baby in the next basket?

GIRL: You mean . . .

BOY: Right! The bed wetter!

GIRL: Oh my goodness, of course! The one who thought he was a girl.

BOY: Well, I was wrong. I'm a boy.

GIRL: Are you sure this time?

BOY: Oh, yeah. I'm a boy.

GIRL: How can you tell?

BOY: I hate girls. Boy, I really hate 'em! They're disgusting! Blechhh! All except Brooke Shields. What a cutie. A real strawberry shortcake. *Crazy* about Brooke Shields! You can have all the rest.

GIRL: *I'm* a girl.

BOY: You're kidding.

GIRL: Do you hate me?

BOY: Wait a minute—no, I don't think so. Hey, you don't suppose it's a new phase I'm going through, do you? I'm going through so many new phases I don't know which end is up. So how's life been treating you?

GIRL: I'm not sure. I'm only a month old.

BOY: Yeah, me, too. The time really drags when you're just lying here, doesn't it? When you think there could be seventy, eighty more years of this, it could get to be a real bummer. What's it like where you live?

GIRL: Things'd be really great if it weren't for two things.

BOY: Yeah? What?

GIRL: My brother and sister.

BOY: What's a brother and sister?

GIRL: You know—people who go around pinching you and sticking their tongues out at you and going *PHUTTT!*
    (Bronx cheer)

BOY: I never heard of such a thing. Why don't you tell them to stop?

GIRL: Are you crazy? I can't talk yet!

BOY: Right. Right. I forgot.

GIRL: Why do you suppose they keep doing those things? I'm not mad at them.

BOY: If you ask me, they're just jealous.

GIRL: Of what?

BOY: Everything! They've got to walk to the park and you get to ride—they've got all those ugly white things in their mouth and you don't—they've got to get up to go to the bathroom and you can do it right where you are—

GIRL: You know something? I think you're right.

BOY: I'm always right. It's a curse. I've been alive one month and already I've been right five times. A *curse*!

GIRL: You were wrong about being a girl . . .

BOY: That was my first try. You get one practice wrong before it counts. What'd you call those terrible people—brother and what?

GIRL: Sister.

BOY: I never heard of such a thing. Where did they come from?

GIRL: I don't know. They were already there when I got home. I think maybe my mother gave birth to them—like she gave birth to me.

BOY: My mother didn't give birth to *any* children. Not even me.

GIRL: What do you mean?

BOY: I was adopted.

GIRL: What's that?

BOY: Remember when your family came to get you at the hospital?

GIRL: Of course.

BOY: Mine let their fingers do the walking.

GIRL: I don't understand.

BOY: They sent away.

GIRL: That sounds weird.

BOY: Are you kidding? It's great! Think of the adventure. They could've ended up with *any*body—a blond one, a dark one, a fat one, a skinny one, one with a dimple, one with a rosebud for a mouth, one with a cute little tush—but what did they get? All of it—me! Your family *had* to take you, no matter what.

GIRL: They didn't do so bad.

BOY: Believe me, you're not such a hot item.

GIRL: That's an awful thing to say!

BOY: What do you expect? I'm too young to be diplomatic. I call 'em like I see 'em.

GIRL: Look—here comes another baby carriage.

NEW GIRL: What you say, momma? What's goin' down, my main man?
Gimme five and that's no jive!

BOY: Look at that—a baby basketball player.

NEW GIRL: Look at *that*—a baby baseball manager.

BOY: What makes you think I'm a baseball manager?

NEW GIRL: What makes you think I'm a basketball player?

BOY: I'm sorry. It's just that I saw you dribbling.
(Explaining)
That's a little joke, you see.

NEW GIRL: Hey, fool, how'd you like me to put one upside your head?

BOY: I don't think I'd like that at all.

GIRL: You're *always* making jokes. I'll bet you want to be a
comedian when you grow up.

BOY: No, I want to be the same thing my father is.
He's an anchorperson.

GIRL: No kidding! Have I seen him? What's he on?

BOY: The *S.S. Morris Greenblatt.*

NEW GIRL: What channel's that?

BOY: The East River.

NEW GIRL: He's an anchorperson on the *East River?*

BOY: Certainly! When the captain shouts "Anchors aweigh!" he pulls it up and off we go.

NEW GIRL: That's all he does?

BOY: What do you mean? It happens to be a very important job.
If he didn't do it, the boat couldn't go anywhere. Of course, it
means he has to be away from home a lot. But when I *do* see
him, he gives me quality time. That's my favorite thing, quality time—that and holding someone's finger.

NEW GIRL: When *I* grow up, I'm gonna be the same thing my *momma* is.

BOY: What's that?

NEW GIRL: A cocktail waitress.

BOY: A cocktail waitress! You're kidding! That's what
I wanted to be! Before I decided to be an anchorperson,
of course.
(Confidentially)
I'll tell you the truth—I *still* want to be a cocktail
waitress. That cute little tray, those fishnet stockings,
all those tips—oo*ee!*
(Once again talking to NEW GIRL)
And how 'bout your *dad?* Is he a cocktail waitress, too?

NEW GIRL: No, he's a dentist.

BOY: A *what*?

NEW GIRL: A dentist. You know—a person you go to when you need your teeth fixed.

BOY: What are teeth?

NEW GIRL: I don't know. They show up later. But if you don't brush 'em twice a day, they go away again.

BOY: Okay, so what we've got here so far, job-wise, is a cocktail waitress, an anchorperson and a dentist. Now what about you?

GIRL: Me? You're talking to me?

BOY: You bet your cute booties. So tell me, what do *your* parents do?

GIRL: Well . . . my mother drives a truck.

BOY: You're kidding! Your mother drives a *truck*?

GIRL: You want to make something of it?

BOY: Well, no, I don't think I do.

GIRL: You want me to put something up—uh—next to your head?

NEW GIRL: Upside your head, darlin'—upside.

GIRL: Yeah, upside your head.

BOY: What are you getting so excited about? I think truck drivers are great! If I can't be an anchorperson or a cocktail waitress, I'm going to drive a truck.

NEW GIRL: And what about your father, darlin'? What's he do?

GIRL: *(Hesitates)* What's a father?

NEW GIRL: You know . . .

GIRL: No, I don't.

NEW GIRL: Sure you do. Remember when you were being born and everybody was running around like crazy and people were doing all sorts of weird stuff, remember that?

GIRL: Yeah . . .

NEW GIRL: Well, the one who was getting nauseous is called a father.

GIRL: We don't have one of them. There's just my mother and my brother and my sister and me.

BOY: That's terrible.

GIRL: No it's not! We have a *good* time, my mom and me. She feeds me and she plays with me and she hugs me and kisses me and she protects me and she tells me I'm beautiful. I *am* beautiful, don't you think?

NEW GIRL: You certainly are. And you want to know why? It's because somebody loves you. It doesn't matter if it's a mom or a pop or a second cousin once removed—long as one person loves you, you're beautiful. That's what my father, the dentist, says.

BOY: Gosh, that's nice. Your father's a regular *philosopher*-dentist.

NEW GIRL: Yeah? What's that?

BOY: How should I know? I'm only one month old.

GIRL: Hey, you know what let's do? Why don't we meet here in the park every day for the rest of our lives?

BOY: Every day? Let me check—I think my calendar's clear. Monday . . . Tuesday . . . yep, every day's fine. How about you?

NEW GIRL: Why not? I got nothin' better to do till I can walk.

GIRL: Okay, then. It's a date.

BOY: My first date! I'm so excited I could stop wetting my pants.

GIRL: I'll bring the apple juice.

NEW GIRL: I'll bring the strained carrots.

BOY: And I'll bring the ribs.

NEW GIRL: What do you know about ribs, fool?

GIRL: Hey, look out. Here come some grown-ups.

NEW GIRL: Uh oh. We don't want *them* messin' in.

BOY: There's only one thing to do. Ready?

GIRL: Ready.

BOY: Goo!

GIRL: Goo!

NEW GIRL: Goo, baby.

A Tale of Three Ralphs

by Miriam Minkowitz
Illustrated by Debra Solomon

Once upon a time there lived a husband and wife who decided that if they ever had children, they would do everything in their power to be the fairest parents in the entire world. "To make sure that we bring up all our children equally fairly," they vowed, "let's make one Golden Rule: EACH CHILD WILL BE TREATED *EXACTLY ALIKE*—WITH ABSOLUTELY *NO EXCEPTIONS.*"

Soon the husband and wife had a little baby son. They named him Ralph, and they loved and cherished him very deeply. He grew and grew, and the little family was incredibly happy.

When Ralph was three years old, his parents had a second child. This time it was a baby girl. Remembering their rule to treat each of their children *exactly alike*—with absolutely *no exceptions*—they named her Ralph also. For a moment, they thought about calling her Ralph the Second.

"But that's not *exactly* what we called our first child," protested the husband.

"You're right," agreed the wife. "It wouldn't be fair." So they decided to call the new baby just plain Ralph.

As time went on, no matter what happened, the parents kept their promise to treat each of their children exactly alike. And so, when their first Ralph developed a runny nose, they gave *both* children nose drops. And when their second Ralph fell down while roller-skating, both children went around with bandaged knees until the second Ralph's cut was completely healed.

Finally, when the first Ralph was ten, and the second Ralph was seven, the proud parents had a third child—a beautiful baby daughter. Naturally enough, they named her Ralph, and soon afterward, they brought her home from the hospital. It was then that the husband and wife first began to notice that their decision to treat each of their children *exactly alike*—with absolutely *no exceptions*—was causing a few problems.

For one thing, since they wanted to keep newborn Ralph in diapers, they had to make the other Ralphs wear diapers as well. And, since newborn Ralph couldn't walk, the parents were forced to make the other Ralphs lie around in cribs all day, just like their baby sister did. Well, the older Ralphs were not altogether pleased with this state of affairs, and they objected quite strenuously. "It's not fair," they yelled from their cribs. "It's just not fair."

The parents thought long and hard about their children's complaints. "How could it not be fair?" they wondered. "After all, we've brought up each of our children exactly alike—with absolutely no exceptions." Finally, the wife came up with a plan. "Maybe it would be better," she suggested, "if, instead of treating the older Ralphs the same as newborn Ralph, we did just the opposite."

"That's absolutely *brilliant,* sweetheart!" enthused the husband. "Let's start right away." And they did.

Over the next few weeks, despite both parents' very best efforts to make the new plan a success, matters really didn't improve much. For example, when they demanded that newborn Ralph set the table and clean up her room, she just burst into tears and did nothing. When the mother requested, "Ralph, please let the cat out," the infant just stuck her thumb in her mouth and dribbled. And when the father grasped the baby gently by her shoulder and said, "Ralph, it's time for school!" she just wrapped her tiny hand around one of his fingers and answered, "Goooooo?"

"What shall we do?" sobbed the poor father in despair.

"I don't know!" wailed the poor mother. "We have a Golden Rule that all our children are to be treated *exactly* alike. And we absolutely *insist* on being fair. I'm afraid there's just no solution."

Finally the oldest Ralph said, "Maybe we can help." His parents looked at him blankly.

"Maybe, just maybe, all us children could be treated exactly alike— *except for certain things.*"

"Except for certain things?" mused their father. "What a curious idea!"

"It *does* sound interesting," added their mother. "But how would it work?"

"Well, suppose that you and Dad treated us exactly alike—*except* when it seemed silly to do so," answered their son.

"Sure," his sister chimed in. "Like when Mom and Dad made us both get braces because *your* front teeth were crooked, that was silly. But when they bought each of us identical Venus flytrap plants—and identical little bags of bugs and ants to feed them—well, *that* was fair."

Their mother looked at her husband and nodded. "I see what they mean," she said.

"And while we're at it," the second Ralph said, "it's silly for all of us to be called 'Ralph.' And confusing, too."

"But what can we possibly do about it *now*?" their father wanted to know.

"Well, you could *start* by giving us new names," the first Ralph suggested.

"Fair enough," said their father.

"Well, why *not*?" said their mother. She turned to the first Ralph. "Ralph, what would you like *your* name to be?"

"Well, I've always been rather partial to the name 'Ralph,' " he said.

"Okay . . ." said the mother uncertainly. " 'Ralph' it is." She looked at the second Ralph. "And how about you?" she said. "If you could have any name in the world, what would you pick?"

"No doubt about it," her daughter replied without hesitation. "I'd like to be called 'Ralph.' "

"Uh-huh," said the father. He looked in the crib where his infant daughter lay chewing on the schoolbooks her parents had left there in the vain hope she would finally begin to catch up on her homework. "And I suppose you'd like us to keep calling *you* Ralph, too?"

The baby was too young to answer, of course, but the parents could tell from the glint in her eye that the name "Ralph" suited her just fine.

And so, from that time on, Ralph, Ralph, and their little sister Ralph faced a fair, but somewhat confusing, future in a family with a *new* Golden Rule for bringing up children equally fairly:

"SINCE NO RALPHS ARE
JUST LIKE THEIR SISTERS
AND BROTHERS,
WHAT'S GOOD FOR ONE RALPH
MIGHT BE BAD FOR
THE OTHERS."

Or, in other words,
"TO EACH RALPH BE TRUE."

Friendly Neighborhood

Words by Lynn Ahrens,
Music by Stephen Flaherty
Illustrated by Lonni Sue Johnson

♪ see page 157 for the music

My family began
with Mom and Dad and Sam and me.
Then Mom and Dad divorced,
and, boy, I cried!
'Cause suddenly, instead of four,
my family felt like three,
and it took a little while
'til Sam and me could see
that what we'd really done was multiplied.

Mom got married to a fella
and I got to catch the flowers at the wedding.
Well, we like him,
and we call him Ted the Bear.
Ted has three kids
from when he used to be the husband of Alicia,
and they visit us on weekends,
and he takes us everywhere.
And let me tell you,
We really have to squish into that car.
It's a tight squeeze.

And Dad met Marsha. She's a lawyer.
And I think they're getting married.
Her two kids are both adopted,
and they come from Vietnam.

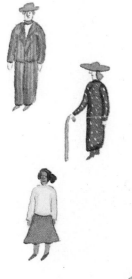

So that makes Mom and Ted the Bear,
and Dad and Marsha and Alicia,
three new brothers, two new sisters,
and my creepy brother Sam.
I think Sam is still a little shy around girls.
Well, he's just little.
I'm older!

And there's Gram,
good old Gram,
and there's Grandpa Henry,
also Grandma Annie,
plus an extra granny,
'cause now there's Grandma Pam.

And I'm not even counting cousins,
'cause by now there must be dozens.
Some are younger, some are older,
I mean, cousins by the ton!
And as for having aunts and uncles,
well, the list would take me hours,
but at holidays and birthdays,
gee, the crowd is really fun!
Except, of course, you
have to get kissed and hugged
a whole lot more. Ugh!

Mom and Dad are doing fine,
And Sam and me are doing fine,
and, hey, we feel a whole lot better
than I ever thought we would!
I mean, okay, my family split,
but now, the pieces kinda fit . . .
and it's like living in the middle of
a friendly neighborhood!
And you know what?
Best thing of all?
They all like me!

Another Cinderella

by Norman Stiles
Illustrated by Ralph Reese

Once upon a time there lived a girl named Cinderella. Not *that* Cinderella. Another Cinderella.

This Cinderella lived with her really nice stepmother, really nice stepsister, and really nice stepbrother. She was the light of their lives. All they wanted was that Cinderella be as happy as a young girl could be.

From the day Cinderella became part of their family, they bent over backward to "give her space" and to "let her do her own thing." They freely and gladly worked their fingers to the bone to give her anything and everything she needed or wanted, and they never, ever made her do *any* chores.

That's right. No chores! Ever! Never!

Not only didn't she have to lift a finger, they would lift it for her.

She didn't have to clean up her room or put her stuff away or even put the cap back on the toothpaste if she didn't feel like it.

She didn't have to help wash the dishes or dry the dishes or bring her dish to the sink or even *use* a dish if she didn't feel like it.

She could do whatever she wanted to do whenever she wanted to do it and they never butted in.

If she didn't feel like it, she didn't have to go to school.

They did her homework for her.

She could eat whenever she was hungry and they would cook it for her no matter what time of day.

She could go to sleep whenever she wanted to go to sleep and get up whenever she wanted to get up.

She could eat in bed . . . even something with gravy!

Of course, she never, ever had to help clean the cinders out of the fireplace. She liked to watch *them* do that. (That's why they called her Cinderella.)

She had it made. What a life!

So how come she cried all the time?

"Who knows? Maybe it's a phase," her stepmother said. "She'll grow out of it . . . I hope."

Of course they tried to talk to her. "Why are you crying?" they would ask.

"I don't know," Cinderella would sob. "I don't know." And she didn't know why she cried. She just couldn't explain it.

"Hey, come on, stop crying," her stepmother would say. "Go out and have some fun! Here's some money. Buy yourself something."

"Eat something."

"Go see a funny play."

"Have your hair done."

"Have your nails done."

"Have a nice cup of tea."

"Have a nice day."

"Whatever it is, try not to think about it."

"Hold your breath and count to twenty. It works with hiccups, maybe it will work with crying."

"Take a trip."

"Take a ride."

"Take an aspirin."

"Take a hot bath."

"Take off a couple of pounds."

Some of these things worked for a little while, but soon, out of nowhere and for no apparent reason, Cinderella would burst into tears again.

Then, one Friday, Cinderella came home from school and said, "I have a book report to write. It's due on Monday."

"A book report? Over the weekend? Oh! You poor dear!" her step-mother said as she arrived home from work.

"Let me do it for you, Cinderella!" the stepbrother cried.

"No, let me!" the stepsister jumped in.

"No. Me!"

"No! Me!"

They argued back and forth.

"Now, now. No fighting, kids. You *both* can do it for her," said Cinderella's stepmother.

"Yay," they yelled as they jumped around happily.

Cinderella burst into tears.

But this time her stepmother offered something very, very special to soothe her. She showed Cinderella a beautiful designer gown that she had bought for her along with the most beautiful and perfect accessories, including an imported pair of hand-blown glass slippers.

Cinderella stopped crying when her stepmother took her outside to see a golden carriage pulled by two gorgeous horses and attended by two very impressive coachpersons.

"You bought all this for me?" Cinderella asked, blowing her nose.

"Well, I bought the gown and the accessories and the shoes. The coach and the horses and the coachpersons are a rental," her stepmother said proudly. "I did all this for you so you can go to the Prince's Ball at the palace on Sunday night. Maybe the Prince will fall in love with you and marry you and make you happy for ever and ever and then you won't cry all the time."

Cinderella burst into tears. At first everybody thought these were tears of joy. But tears of joy don't usually last from just before supper Friday night until breakfast Sunday morning, with no sign of letting up.

While they worried that Cinderella might cry all day and not be able to go to the ball that night, a great wind began to blow outside their cottage. It

blew louder and louder and stronger, shaking the cottage until finally it blew open the front door and then stopped blowing, all at once.

It was strangely calm and quiet, and they all stared at the open door, not knowing what to expect.

Then, from behind them, they heard, "Made you look! Made you look!"

It was Cinderella's Fairy Godmother. "Came in through the window! I love the unexpected," she said with a twinkle in her eye. "Hi! I'm your Fairy Godmother, and I'm here to help with this crying business."

Everyone was thrilled, including Cinderella. *Especially* Cinderella! It wasn't a lot of fun going through life crying all the time. "How are you going to do it? Wave your magic wand and my crying will stop?" Cinderella wondered.

"No, sweetheart," replied the Fairy Godmother patiently. "I'm good, but I'm not *that* good. And even if I could do that, I'm not sure it would be such a good idea."

"I know. You'll wave your magic wand and bring her a Prince who will make her happy and her crying will stop," offered the stepbrother.

"No. I could conjure up a Prince or two, but it wouldn't work anyway."

"Then you'll wave your wand and bring Cinderella riches beyond her dreams and that will make her crying stop," the stepsister said.

"No. That wouldn't work either."

"Then what *will* you do?" the stepmother demanded impatiently.

"Look," said the Fairy Godmother, "I think that what Cinderella needs is a sense of achievement, a feeling of accomplishment, and the satisfaction that comes from meeting a challenge."

"Oh, I see. You're going to wave your magic wand and give her all that," said the stepmother. "Please hurry. We want the red in her eyes to clear up in time for the ball."

"No. She's going to get all that on her own . . . once she is given some reasonable guidelines and compassionate guidance," the Fairy Godmother said.

"Ah, ha! That must be where the wand comes in," said the stepmother.

"No. That's where *you* come in."

Everyone was very confused. Was she going to use that wand or wasn't she?

She was. And she did. First she waved it and turned the gown into overalls, the glass slippers into work boots, the coach into a pumpkin, and the coachpersons into mice. She left the horses as they were to graze peacefully in the yard.

Everyone except the horses was very upset. A Fairy Godmother wasn't supposed to take things away. What kind of Fairy Godmother was she anyway?

"Relax!" she said. "I'm not finished." And she waved her wand and out of thin air produced a piece of paper and a pencil. It was a very nice piece of paper and a good pencil with a sharp point, but what did a pencil and paper have to do with anything?

The Fairy Godmother explained that she would help Cinderella's stepmother make a list of things Cinderella would have to accomplish before the gown and the other stuff would be restored. If she finished doing everything on the list before it was time to go to the ball, so be it. If not, no ball.

They didn't like it. It didn't sound fair or nice or kind or loving. The Fairy Godmother assured them that it was all of the above. She turned to Cinderella and said, "Just do your best, dear. It will work out. Trust me."

"Okay," Cinderella said in a surprisingly strong voice. "I'll try."

So her stepmother, with the help of the Fairy Godmother, made up the list. It was a pretty long list, too, with things like helping with the breakfast dishes, including bringing her dish to the sink; cleaning up her room by herself; helping with the laundry; etc. She even had to do her book report all by herself.

One by one Cinderella did the things on the list, and as she did, she began to feel and look happier and happier. As the day went by, she didn't cry once. It looked like her Fairy Godmother was right. But Cinderella still hadn't written the book report.

"Let us help her," the stepsister begged.

"No," said the stepmother firmly. "I think we should let her do it by herself."

Cinderella's Fairy Godmother smiled because she knew that Cinderella's stepmother was finally getting the picture.

Cinderella smiled, too, and then she wrote and wrote and paced and paced and wrote and erased and wrote some more and finally, with just one hour left before the ball, she finished the book report. She couldn't believe how good she felt. She had never felt that good in her entire life!

Everyone cheered as her Fairy Godmother waved her wand and restored the gown and the glass slippers and the accessories and the coach and the coachpersons.

Cinderella started to cry.

But this time she knew why. She didn't want to go to the ball if it meant she had to marry the Prince. She didn't feel she was ready to get married. She had a lot of things she wanted to do first, like go to school, learn things, grow, become a person, stuff like that.

Her stepmother agreed with her and promised that one thing she didn't have to do if she didn't feel like doing it was marry someone she didn't feel like marrying. The only things she would be expected to do from now on were things like homework and chores and stuff like *that*.

"This calls for a celebration!" the Fairy Godmother said. "And what better place to celebrate than at a ball! Off you go!"

And off they went.

And they had a great time. Cinderella danced with the Prince and thought he was sort of cute and nice. She wanted to stay late, but she left early because she had school the next day and because her stepmother told her it was time to go home.

She did leave her glass slipper behind with the Prince because it had her name and address inside and she wanted to see him again. Besides, she knew where *he* lived so it was only fair.

Over the years Cinderella grew into a fine young woman who wrote book reports for a living. She and the Prince became very good friends, fell in love, got married, and they had a very nice life together.

Cinderella still cried once in a while but, then, so does everybody.

Little Abigail and the Beautiful Pony

Written and Illustrated by Shel Silverstein

There was a girl named Abigail
Who was taking a drive
Through the country
With her parents
When she spied a beautiful sad-eyed
Grey and white pony.
And next to it was a sign
That said,
FOR SALE—CHEAP.
"Oh," said Abigail,
"May I have that pony?
May I please?"
And her parents said,
"No you may not."
And Abigail said,
"But I MUST have that pony."
And her parents said,
"Well, you can't have that pony,
But you can have a nice butter pecan
Ice cream cone when we get home."

And Abigail said,
"I don't want a butter pecan
Ice cream cone,
**I WANT THAT PONY—
I MUST HAVE THAT PONY.**"
And her parents said,
"Be quiet and stop nagging—
You're *not* getting that pony."
And Abigail began to cry and said,
"If I don't get that pony I'll die."
And her parents said, "You won't die.
No child ever died yet from not getting a pony."
And Abigail felt so bad
That when they got home she went to bed,
And she couldn't eat,
And she couldn't sleep,
And her heart was broken,
And she DID die—
All because of a pony
That her parents wouldn't buy.

(This is a good story
To read to your folks
When they won't buy
You something you want.)

33

Some Things Don't Make Any Sense at All

by Judith Viorst
Illustrated by Debra Solomon

My mom says I'm her sugarplum.
My mom says I'm her lamb.
My mom says I'm completely perfect
Just the way I am.
My mom says I'm a super-special wonderful terrific little guy.
My mom just had another baby.
Why?

Stevie

Written and Illustrated by John Steptoe

One day my momma told me, "You know you're gonna have a little friend come stay with you."

And I said, "Who is it?"

And she said, "You know my friend Mrs. Mack? Well, she has to work all week and I'm gonna keep her little boy."

I asked, "For how long?"

She said, "He'll stay all week and his mother will come pick him up on Saturdays."

The next day the doorbell rang. It was a lady and a kid. He was smaller than me. I ran to my mother. "Is that them?"

They went in the kitchen but I stayed out in the hall to listen.

The little boy's name was Steven but his mother kept calling him Stevie. My name is Robert but my momma don't call me Robertie.

And so Steve moved in, with his old crybaby self. He always had to have his way. And he was greedy too. Everything he sees he wants. "Could I have somma that? Gimme this." Man!

Since he was littler than me, while I went to school he used to stay home and play with my toys.

I wished his mother would bring somma *his* toys over here to break up.

I used to get so mad at my mother when I came home after school. "Momma, can't you watch him and tell him to leave my stuff alone?"

Then he used to like to get up on my bed to look out the window and leave his dirty footprints all over my bed. And my momma never said nothin' to him.

And on Saturdays when his mother comes to pick him up, he always tries to act cute just cause his mother is there.

He picked up my airplane and I told him not to bother it. He thought I wouldn't say nothin' to him in front of his mother.

I could never go anywhere without my mother sayin' "Take Stevie with you now."

"But why I gotta take him everywhere I go?" I'd say.

"Now if you were stayin' with someone you wouldn't want them to treat you mean," my mother told me. "Why don't you and Stevie try to play nice?"

Yeah, but I always been nice to him with his old spoiled self. He's always gotta have his way anyway.

I had to take him out to play with me and my friends.

"Is that your brother, Bobby?" they'd ask me.

"No."

"Is that your cousin?"

"No! He's just my friend and he's stayin' at my house and my mother made me bring him."

"Ha, ha. You gotta baby-sit! Bobby the baby-sitter!"

"Aw, be quiet. Come on, Steve. See! Why you gotta make all my friends laugh for?"

"Ha, ha. Bobby the baby-sitter," my friends said.

"Hey, come on, y'all, let's go play in the park. You comin', Bobby?" one of my friends said.

"Naw, my momma said he can't go in the park cause the last time he went he fell and hurt his knee, with his old stupid self."

And then they left.

"You see? You see! I can't even play with my friends. Man! Come on."

"I'm sorry, Robert. You don't like me, Robert? I'm sorry," Stevie said.

"Aw, be quiet. That's okay," I told him.

One time when my daddy was havin' company I was just sittin' behind the couch just listenin' to them talk and make jokes and drink beer. And I wasn't makin' no noise. They didn't even know I was there!

Then here comes Stevie with his old loud self. Then when my father heard him, he yelled at *me* and told me to go upstairs.

Just cause of Stevie.

Sometimes people get on your nerves and they don't mean it or nothin' but they just bother you. Why I gotta put up with him? My momma only had one kid. I used to have a lot of fun before old stupid came to live with us.

One Saturday Steve's mother and father came to my house to pick him up like always. But they said that they were gonna move away and that Stevie wasn't gonna come back anymore.

So then he left. The next mornin' I got up to watch cartoons and I fixed two bowls of corn flakes. Then I just remembered that Stevie wasn't here.

Sometimes we had a lot of fun runnin' in and out of the house. Well, I guess my bed will stay clean from now on. But that wasn't so bad. He couldn't help it cause he was stupid.

I remember the time I ate the last piece of cake in the breadbox and blamed it on him.

We used to play Cowboys and Indians on the stoop.

I remember when I was doin' my homework I used to try to teach him what I had learned. He could write his name pretty good for his age.

I remember the time we played boogie man and we hid under the covers with Daddy's flashlight.

And that time we was playin' in the park under the bushes and we found these two dead rats and one was brown and one was black.

And him and me and my friends used to cook mickies or marshmallows in the park.

We used to have some good times together.

I think he liked my momma better than his own, cause he used to call his mother "Mother" and he called my momma "Mommy."

Aw, no! I let my corn flakes get soggy thinkin' about him.

He was a nice little guy.

He was kinda like a little brother.

Little Stevie.

I'll Fix Anthony

by Judith Viorst
Illustrated by Arnold Lobel

My brother Anthony
can read books now,

but he won't read
any books to me.

He plays checkers
with Bruce
from his school.
But when
I want to play
he says Go away or I'll clobber you.

I let him wear
my Snoopy sweat shirt,
but he never lets me
borrow his sword.

Mother says deep down
in his heart Anthony loves me.

Anthony says deep down
in his heart he thinks I stink.

Mother says deep deep down
in his heart,
where he doesn't even know it,
Anthony loves me.

Anthony says
deep deep down
in his heart he still thinks I stink.

When I'm six
I'll fix Anthony.

When I'm six a dog
will follow me home,

and she'll beg for me and roll over
and lick my face.

If Anthony tries to pet her,
she'll give him a bite.

When I'm six Anthony will have
the German measles,

and my father will take me
to a baseball game.

Then Anthony will have
the mumps,

and my mother will take me
to the flower show.

Then Anthony will have a virus,
and my grandfather
will take me to the movies.

I won't have to save popcorn
for Anthony unless I want to.

When I'm six we'll have
a skipping contest,
and I'll skip faster.

Then we'll have
a jumping contest,
and I'll jump higher.

Then we'll do
Eeny-Meeny-Miney-Mo,
and Anthony will be O-U-T.
He'll be very M-A-D.

When I'm six I'll read

Anthony will still
    be reading

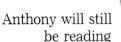

Who are you voting for, Anthony?
I'll ask him.

When I'm six I'll stand
on my head,
and my legs won't wobble.

Anthony's legs
will wobble a lot.

If someone tickles me,
I'll keep standing
on my head.

If someone pinches me,
I'll keep standing
on my head.

If someone says
Give up or I'll clobber you,
I'll keep standing on my head.
Anthony will give up at tickles.
When I'm six I'll know
how to sharpen pencils.

Here's how you do it,
Anthony, I'll say.

When I'm six I'll float,
but Anthony will sink
to the bottom.
I'll dive off the board,
but Anthony will change his mind.

I'll breathe in and out when I should,
but Anthony will only go

When I'm six I'll be tall, and Anthony
will be short because I'll eat things
like carrots and potatoes,
and he'll eat things like
jelly beans and root beer.

I'll put his red sneakers
on the top shelf, and if
he stands on a chair,
he still won't be able
to reach them.

He'll tell me
Get down
my sneakers,
and I'll tell him
Say please,

and if he doesn't say
please, he can't have
his sneakers
for a hundred
years.

When I'm six I'll add
7 and 4 and 10 and 3
inside my mind.

Anthony will just add 1 and 1 and 2,
and he'll have to use
his fingers.

When I'm six we'll have a race,
and I'll be at the corner when Anthony
hasn't even passed the fireplug.

The next time I'll give him
a head start, but it won't help.

When I'm six friends will call me
on the telephone.

No one will call Anthony.
I'll sleep at Charlie's
house and Eddie's and Diana's, but
Anthony will always sleep at home.

See you later, Anthony, I'll tell him.

When I'm six
I'll help people
carry their groceries
from the supermarket,

and they'll say
My, you're strong.

I don't think Anthony
will be strong enough.

When I'm six
I'll be able to tell
left and right,
but Anthony
will be all mixed up.

I'll be able
to tell time,
but Anthony
will be all mixed up.

I'll be able to tell my street and
my city and sometimes my zip code,
but Anthony will be all mixed up.

If he ever gets lost,
I guess I'll have to go find him.

When I'm six Anthony will still be falling
off his bike.

I'll ride by with no hands.

Still falling off that bike?
I'll ask Anthony.

When I'm six I'll let Dr. Ross
look down my throat
with a stick.

If he has to give me
a shot, I won't
even holler.

Try to be brave like your brother,
Dr. Ross will tell Anthony.

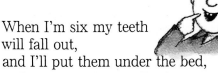

But Anthony won't.

When I'm six my teeth
will fall out,
and I'll put them under the bed,
and the tooth fairy will take
them away and leave dimes.

Anthony's teeth
won't fall out.

He'll wiggle and wiggle them,
but they won't
fall out.

I might sell him one of my teeth,
but I might not.

I'll win all the tic-tac-toes if I'm *X*,
and I'll win them all if I'm *O*.
Too bad, Anthony, I'll say.

Anthony is chasing me out
of the playroom.

He says I stink.
He says he is going to clobber me.
I have to run now, but I won't
have to run when I'm six.

When I'm six
I'll fix Anthony.

When I'm six I'll go BINGO all the time.
Anthony won't even go BINGO once.

It's Not My Fault

Words and Music by
Sarah Durkee and Christopher Cerf
Illustrated by Gary Zamchick

♪ see page 159 for the music

Mom and Dad are mad tonight,
The dinner table's silent,
My sister's gettin' crabby and
My brother's gettin' violent!
Things are lookin' bad tonight,
It's really plain to see,
And I don't know just who's to blame,
But don't go blamin' *me*!

'Cause it's not my fault!
No, it's not my fault!
My family bit my head off,
And all I said was "Pass the salt!"
Hey, it's not my fault!
No, it's not my fault!
When no one else is talkin',
I just tell myself it's not my fault!

Maybe I should tell a joke,
Make everybody laugh,
But every time I tell one
I forget the second half!
Maybe they're all sick of me
For bein' such a jerk,
Or maybe Dad's just tired,
Maybe Mom's just overworked?

Well, it's not my fault!
No, it's not my fault
That no one's sayin' nothin'
'Cause they don't have nothin' nice to say!
Hey, it's not my fault!
No, it's not my fault!
When no one else is talkin',
I just tell myself that I'm okay!

You might be being perfect,
Might be actin' good as gold,
But sometimes people fight no matter *what* you try to do!
We catch each other's anger
Like we catch each other's cold.
That's when you got to tell yourself it's not because of you!

It's not my fault!
No, it's not my fault!
I know I'm not the one
Who put my family in a rotten mood!
Yeah, it's not my fault!
No, it's not my fault!
And just because we're fighting
Doesn't mean we're gonna come unglued!

Well, it's not my fault!
No, it's not my fault!

The Right Family

by Sarah Durkee
Illustrated by Jacqueline Rogers

I hate my family. I know that's bad to say but they deserve it. Nobody ever pays any attention to me unless they're screaming at me, which is usually for no reason. Like just five minutes ago, my sister Chrissie went into hysterics and punched me just because by mistake I waved my arm and got a *tiny* pen mark you can hardly even see with a microscope on her David Lee Roth poster! So of course my mom hears us fighting and comes upstairs yelling her head off about us breaking the house rule of no loud noise when she's working. And then of course my baby brother Jake wakes up crying and Mom rushes off to check on him just when I'm starting to explain what happened, and she says she'll talk to me later, but my stepfather comes home any minute and then they'll start making dinner so she'll probably forget. It seems like that's the way it almost *always* is around here lately. What I have to say just isn't important to anybody.

So now I'm standing here rubbing the microscopic pen mark off the David Lee Roth poster with a pen eraser, even though Chrissie screamed that pen erasers never work, and she went stomping out of our room to go call her stupid friend Erica to tell her how much she hates me, probably, and while I'm erasing I figure it out. I'm in the wrong family.

I'm sure that must happen sometimes. Mistakes happen. A girl and her family are completely wrong for each other, and she's trying to fit in with them but they just don't mix. Like gum with chocolate. It doesn't work. So the girl just goes and finds another family, no hard feelings.

Then I start picturing in my head what it would be like if these people in my family have always *thought* I'm related to them but it turns out I'm not. My name isn't Annie Ferber, it's MIRANDA MARTINDALE, and I'm just here to visit. If I were just a guest here visiting, they'd be really nice. They'd give me matching clean towels to use, and ask me how I like my burger cooked, and if I have any hobbies and what my favorite TV shows are, and everyone would listen. Closely. And they'd laugh when I say something funny, and when I have a good idea they'd remember that it was mine even when Chrissie says the same thing two seconds later.

And then they'd ask, "What's *your* family like, Miranda?"

They'd have big smiles on their faces, like you use for guests, waiting for my answer. . . .

Oh *no!* Something terrible has happened. The pen mark is gone, but I've rubbed the color off the poster completely!! David Lee Roth's nose now has a big white spot on it! Chrissie is going to be *unbelievably* mad. I get my crayons out of the desk drawer. I decide APRICOT matches the best even though it's a little weird. I start coloring in the white spot. It'll be fine.

45

So anyway, they say, "What's *your* family like, Miranda?"

First I tell them about my mother. Her name is Penelope Martindale and she's very famous. She is very, very beautiful like Cybill Shepherd and she is an expert horseback rider and singer. I travel around the world with her most of the year winning trophies and singing in nightclubs, so of course I can't be in regular school but I learn many foreign languages just by talking to people when we go to fancy restaurants. We talk about *everything,* and she says, "Why Miranda, we're best friends! You can call me Penelope." It's just her and me when we travel because my sister was ordered by the government to go to a special military school in Iowa that's very strict. There aren't even any phones. We haven't seen her in years. I sent her some candy from Switzerland once just because I felt sorry for her.

Oops. The big white spot on the poster is now sort of the color of a mango. There's this big waxy dot of mango color in the middle of David Lee Roth's nose. It looks *really* bad. Jake is still screaming in the other room, which usually drives me nuts but at least it means Mom won't come in right now. Back to the Crayola box . . . maybe it needs a little CARNATION PINK. If Chrissie comes back before I finish fixing this, she'll *kill* me.

Where was I? Oh, so they say, "Isn't that interesting, Annie! I mean, Miranda! You're such a fascinating guest! Tell us more!"

So I tell them about my father. His name is Clint Martindale.

I tell them how when my mother and I come back from our trips around the world my father meets us at the airport in his red convertible. He hugs us and says, "Penelope! Miranda! You look radiant!" My father is the Mayor of California and everyone knows him and loves him. He says, "Would you care to drive, Miranda?" and I drive us to Hollywood with the top down and we visit Lionel Richie and drink drinks. Then we visit Cher. Then we go home to our beautiful California mansion with a pool and take a dip. Later on they throw a huge political party for us because my father has done so many important things. Lionel Richie is there. Then we get up on a stage and my mother and father kiss and announce that our family is perfect and they're never going to have another baby. Everyone cheers.

Uh-oh. David Lee Roth now looks like Bozo the Clown! I keep making it worse and worse when I try to blend it in! I'm starting to panic. If Chrissie sees this, I'm really dead. How could I be so dumb?! She'll never forgive me! She'll never believe I was just trying to fix it! I shouldn't have used the crayons. . . . Maybe if I sort of scraped some of it off? That's it. It's too shiny. I get one of Chrissie's nail files and scrape it a little bit. . . . There, that looks a little better. I keep scraping. I wish I'd never been born!

Jake finally stops crying and starts giggling. Mom must be tickling his belly. Babies sure get a lot of attention . . . and since they can't really *do* anything, they can't really do anything *wrong*. . . .

Like what I just did, for instance! My hand slipped! I just ripped right through David Lee Roth's nose into the wall!! *There's now a big hole in the middle of his face!!*
I might as well give up. It's completely ruined. This is the worst thing I've ever done. Chrissie will scream about how this is a perfect example of why she needs her own room and I'll have to share with Jake. My stepfather will take my side, but only because he feels sorry for me because he thinks I'm just upset about a lot of other things and I'm NOT! And besides it's none of his business. And my mom will just look at me like she's kind of surprised and disappointed and that's the worst of all. I wish I were Miranda Martindale. This would NEVER happen to her. I wish I were Chrissie . . . I wish I were *Jake* . . . I wish I were ANYBODY but me right now. I wish I could vaporize.
I can hear Chrissie saying good-bye to Erica on the phone downstairs!! This is it. She'll murder me. She's coming any second and there's nowhere to run—maybe if I stand in front of it??? Oh please please please please please don't let her see it!!! I yank the poster down from the wall without even knowing what I'm going to do! Jump out the window with it?! Hide it?! Crumple it up and eat it??! *I can hear her footsteps!!!* HERE SHE COMES!!!
Chrissie walks in and I'm standing frozen stiff in the middle of the room with the poster in my hands. She starts freaking out the minute she sees it.
"What did you DO??" she howls at me. "My POSTER! What did you DO??"
I can't even talk. She's about a foot taller than me. She's scary.
"LOOK at this!" she screams, pointing at the hole. "What did you DO?? I leave the room for five minutes and you WRECK everything!! What did you *DO?!!*"
Her voice is getting higher and crazier. Her eyes are bugging out of her head.
I've got nothing to lose.
I lift up the poster and stick my nose through the hole.
"I AM DAVID LEE ROTH!!" I groan. I start walking toward her like a zombie.
"CUT IT OUT!" Chrissie yells, but she's trying not to laugh. I must look pretty great. "What did you *DO?!*" she screeches again.
I go after her. It's my only hope. "AAAAAAAGH!!!" I scream. "I AM DAVID LEE RAWWWWWTH!!" and I start chasing her around the room.
"CUT IT OUT!! CUT IT *OUT!!*" Chrissie yells.
"I AM DAVID LEE RAWWWWWTH!!"
Now we're *definitely* breaking the no-loud-noise rule. My stepfather pokes his head in and Mom rushes in holding Jake. Jake looks at me chasing Chrissie around

the room screaming with a poster over my face and thinks it's the funniest thing he's ever seen.

But I bet Mom won't think it's very funny.

"AN-*NIE!!*" Chrissie pleads. I've got her pinned against the bookshelf. She's sort of laughing and crying at the same time. I step back. Chrissie pulls herself together. No way is she going to let me off easy. "Mom, look what she did to my POSTER!!"

"She's being David Lee Roth?" my stepfather asks Mom calmly. He's almost always calm. I like that about him all of a sudden. I take the poster off my nose.

"She DESTROYED my POSTER!!" Chrissie shouts.

Mom is trying to look mad but she looks sort of happy. She looks happy at the weirdest times. She shifts Jake to her other hip. "What *happened,* Annie?"

It's really quiet. Everybody's listening to me. I can't *remember* the last time I was the center of attention like this. But Chrissie is glaring at me. This kind of attention is not so hot. "Well . . ." I start.

My voice sounds tiny. I decide to keep it simple and get it over with.

"I tried to erase the pen mark but I made it worse and worse. I'm sorry, Chrissie. I'm really sorry. I was only trying to fix it."

Mom ruffles my hair. She's crazy about honesty. "Mistakes happen," she says. "But next time could you make them a little more *quietly*?"

Everyone watches Chrissie. She takes the poster from me and looks it over closely with this really sad face. Then I see her trying not to smile again. I know Chrissie really well.

"Annie?" she says softly.

"What," I say. I'm still scared.

She sticks her nose through the hole in the poster, yells "I AM DAVID LEEEEE RAWWWWWWTH!!!!" right in my face, and starts chasing me around the room screaming and laughing.

She forgives me! I can't *believe* she forgives me, but she does!

My parents and Jake crack up.

Forget the Martindales.

I'm definitely in the right family.

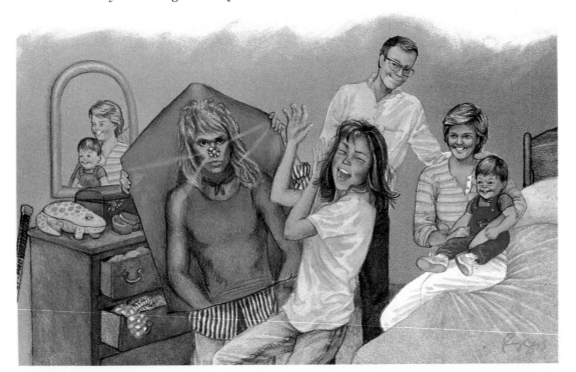

Crowded Tub

Written and Illustrated by Shel Silverstein

There's too many kids in this tub.
There's too many elbows to scrub.
I just washed a behind
That I'm sure wasn't mine,
There's too many kids in this tub.

In My Room

Words and Music by Bobby Gosh
Illustrated by Petra Mathers

♪ see page 160 for the music

There's a place where I love to be
Far away from my family,
And it's near enough so I'm right close by their side.
There's a place I can call my own
When I'm sad and want to be alone,
Or when I'm happy or when I just need a place to hide.

In my room, in my room,
In my own very special room,
I can always find a place
To call my room.
It can be most anywhere,
Under a table or behind a chair,
And my favorite place to be
Is in my room.

Sometimes my mom or dad
Will make me a little mad,
Then I need a place to be with only me.
I'll make believe I'm a rock 'n' roll star
And maybe play a little air guitar
Or read awhile or maybe watch TV.

In my room, in my room,
In my own very special room,
I can be anyone I want to be
In my room.
I can do anything I dare
And pretend that I'm anywhere,
Yes, my favorite place to be
Is in my room.

Some people don't read the sign
That says this place is mine,
Please knock before you enter my own room.
Then I might say, "Come on in!
How're you doin'? Where've you been?
Make yourself at home here in my room!"

In my room, in my room,
In my own very special room,
I can be anyone I want to be
In my room.
I can do anything I dare
And pretend that I'm anywhere,
Yes, my favorite place to be
Is in my room.

My Grandma

by Letty Cottin Pogrebin
Illustrated by Susan Stillman

I used to be ashamed of my Grandma.

I know that's a terrible thing to say, but it was true until last Wednesday, so I have to admit it.

My Grandma lives in our basement.

She moved in about a year ago after Grandpa died. Mom and Dad put a Chinese screen in front of the water heater and stuck a blue rug on the floor, so it looks pretty nice for a basement. Grandma says she can be happy anywhere as long as she has a hard bed and her exercise bike.

My Grandma loves her exercise bike. She rides for twenty minutes every day and she's almost seventy. She makes me ride for ten minutes because she says I'm only half as strong as she is even if I'm sixty years younger.

"A sound mind needs a sound body," she says. But she talks funny so it comes out *a zound mind nids a zound body.*

My Grandma is from the Old Country. When I was little, I thought that was just a nice way of saying she was *old*, but it means she wasn't born here. She grew up speaking Yiddish and Polish and Hungarian and I forget what else, but whatever it was, it definitely makes her English sound weird. That's just *one* of the things I used to get embarrassed about.

At first I was glad she moved in because she's kind of fun to be with. She lets me braid her long gray hair, and she teaches me things like gin rummy and knitting and how to make those little pastries with nuts and sugar rolled up in them. She calls them *rugalach.* I can't say it as well as she does so I call them ruggies.

I used to love Grandma's stories, too.

No matter what we're doing, she always slaps her forehead and says "Oy, that reminds me of a story."

One time when we were baking, she remembered how she once churned butter so long it turned to cheese. "I was daytime dreaming," she said with a laugh.

And once we were sewing and my scissors wouldn't cut, and she told me about this guy who used to ride through the streets of her town with a special cart with a sharpener.

"He made a clang on his cowbell," she said, "and we ran out from our houses with our dull knives and scissors, and he sharpened them on a big stone wheel. Such sparks you never saw."

I told her that sounded pretty neat. I wish we had one of those guys in our neighborhood.

When there's a full moon outside, my Grandma always pulls down the window shades near my bed. She says it's bad luck if the moon shines on you when you sleep. I make fun of her superstitions but she always says, "You never know . . . you never know."

Mostly, my Grandma's stories are funny. But sometimes they're scary—so scary that I have to scrunch up my shoulders to cover my ears, even if I've heard them before.

For instance, there's the one about her aunt and uncle who lived in this poor little town with a winding brook and a wooden bridge. It sounds like she's starting a fairy tale but I know she's working up to the part about the pogroms. That's when these soldiers called Cossacks attacked and burned Jewish people's houses. We're Jewish.

"If it wasn't for the pogroms," she says, "a lot of Jews who ran away to America would have stayed in Europe. Then they would have been killed by the Nazis. So maybe the pogroms were a blessing in disguise."

To me that's like saying, "Good thing we were hit by a two-ton bus or we might've been flattened by a ten-ton truck."

But to Grandma it's a happy ending. Grandma *loves* happy endings.

The trouble started when my friend Katy found Grandma's false teeth floating in a glass on the bathroom sink. I guess I was so used to seeing them that I didn't even notice them anymore. But Katy noticed. She shouted, "Yuuuck! Gross!" and started laughing hysterically, and pretending to talk to them and making them talk back. I had to get down on my knees and *beg* her to shut up so my grandmother wouldn't hear and get her feelings hurt.

After that happened, I started to realize there were a *million* things about Grandma that were embarrassing. Like the way she grabs my face in her palms and murmurs "*Shaine maidel*" which means "beautiful girl" in Yiddish. What would Katy say if she saw *that*!

Or how Grandma always says her *B'rachas* before she eats. *B'rachas* are Hebrew blessings that thank God for things. All I can say is my Grandma must really be hungry because what she eats isn't exactly worth a thank-you note. Chopped herring is gross enough but white bread soaking in warm milk could make a regular person throw up.

And that's just the problem. My friends are regular people. So when Katy or Jill or Angie are around, I have to worry about what Grandma's going to do next.

Once she took me and Jill out to Burger King, even though she doesn't eat there herself because they don't have kosher meat. Instead of ordering our hamburgers well done, she told the person behind the counter "They'll have two Whoppers well-to-do." Jill burst out laughing, but I almost died.

Another thing I spend half my life explaining is why my Grandma wears a wig. It's not a designer wig either. It's like the hair on an old doll, sort of frizzy and brownish.

I have to explain that she doesn't wear it because her hair fell out and she doesn't wear it to change her hairdo. She wears it because the Jewish law she believes in says that after a woman gets married, she's not allowed to show her own hair to anyone but her husband.

"But he died," Katy said. "So what does he care now?"

Some things you just can't explain.

After a while, I started wishing I could hide my Grandma in a closet. It got so bad I even complained to my parents.

"You guys are at work all afternoon! You don't know what it's *like*. She barges in and talks nonstop. She tries to teach us thousand-year-old games that aren't even in English. And she looks like the Grandmother From Another Planet."

My parents said they understood how I felt, but I had to be careful not to make Grandma feel unwelcome in our house.

"She's had a very tough life," said my Dad.

"Try to make the best of it," said my Mom.

I was trying, *believe* me, I was trying.

Then, like I told you, on Wednesday, something happened that changed everything. My teacher made an announcement that our school was going to be a part of a big Oral History Project. We were supposed to help find interesting old people and interview them about their lives so kids in the future will understand how things used to be.

I was trying to think if I knew anyone interesting when Angie nudged me from across the aisle.

"Volunteer your grandmother!" she whispered.

I was shocked.

"My Grandma??" I said.

"Yeah!" Angie said. "*She's* interesting!"

Interesting? That's the *last* thing I ever thought Angie would say about Grandma!

Well, okay, I said to myself. Why not? Talking is what my Grandma likes to do best. In fact, I've never been able to get her to stop.

So that's how I ended up here. The whole school is in the auditorium for a big assembly and I'm up here on the stage interviewing my own Grandma.

We have microphones clipped to our shirts and TV cameras pointed at us and a bunch of professors are standing off to the side in case I need help asking questions.

Which I don't.

After all this time, nobody knows my Grandma's stories better than I do. I just say the right thing to get her started.

Like when I say "Grandma, why did you leave the Old Country?" she goes right into how the Nazis took over her town.

I've heard all that before. But then she starts telling this incredible story that is brand new to me:

"My parents, they sold all their furniture to buy passage to America. In the meantime, they hid me in a broken-down barn under a pile of straw.

"Can you believe it?" Grandma says looking right at me. "When I was only a little older than you are now, I was running from the Nazis. Me and my parents and my grandparents got into a big old ship, and people were getting sick during the trip and some of them even died. But we had a happy ending when we saw the Statue of Liberty."

While my Grandma talks, I see all my friends and teachers are listening to her as if she's a great hero. And suddenly I feel so proud of my Grandma, I could burst.

I can hardly wait to ask her the next question.

"How did it feel when you saw the Statue of Liberty, Grandma?"

"Very nice," she says. "When that lady she held up her lamp for us to come in nice and safe, I *knew* everything would be okay. I *knew* it."

Next she talks about her life in America and I hear her saying something else that she never put in any of her stories before. She's telling us that she loved her family very much, but she has to admit one thing: that she used to be ashamed of her grandmother.

"For twenty years that woman was in this country, but she wouldn't learn English never," says my Grandma about her Grandma. "Such a shame she was to me in front of my American girlfriends."

I can't believe my ears. I feel a little stabbing pain in my heart. And right there on the stage I make a *B'racha* to thank God for never letting my Grandma know I was ashamed of her, too.

"Thank you for sharing your experiences—the happy ones and the painful ones," the principal is saying to Grandma. "We're so glad your granddaughter brought you to us today."

Everyone starts clapping really loud. I feel like laughing and crying at the same time. I feel like hugging my Grandma and saying I'm sorry and nominating her for the Grammy Award for Grandmothers.

But I just stand on the stage and listen to the applause, and I feel my Grandma grip my hand tight as we take our bows together.

AND SUPERBOY MAKES 3

WRITTEN BY
MARK SALTZMAN

"AS FOR HOW I WAS *ADOPTED*-- WELL, MY PARENTS TOLD ME ALL ABOUT IT."

39 JMNI

THREE YEARS! WE'VE WAITED *THREE YEARS*, AND NOW THEY TELL US WE HAVE TO *KEEP* WAITING!

THESE ADOPTION AGENCIES TAKE SO MUCH TIME!

"BUT THEY WANTED A CHILD SO BADLY. AND THEY KEPT ON *HOPING*."

PENCILS: *CARMINE INFANTINO*
INKS: *DICK GIORDANO*
COLORS: *ADRIENNE ROY*
EDITOR: *JOE ORLANDO*
LETTERER: *HELEN VESIK*

I GUESS WE'VE JUST GOT TO BE *PATIENT*, MARTHA. AFTER ALL...

SCREEECH!

JONATHAN, YOU'RE JUST NOT GOING TO *BELIEVE* THIS!

The Entertainer

by Jeff Moss
Illustrated by Chris Demarest

When Elizabeth was not quite three
She learned to say her A–B–C
Both frontward and backward, either way
From A to Z and Z to A.
Well, Lizzie's mom and her father, too,
Were very proud of what Liz could do,
So they gave a small party in their house in the lane
And invited some friends to watch Liz entertain.
"You'll see," said her father, while cutting the cake,
"She'll go forward and backward without a mistake!"
"We're so proud," said her mom, "of our smart little kid.
Say the alphabet, Lizzie!" And Elizabeth did.
She messed up on L and reversed J and K,
And her parents' friends giggled from Z back to A.
And though everyone clapped when young Lizzie was done,
For Liz, the experience wasn't much fun.
"It's strange," Lizzie thought. "They just tell me, 'Go to it!'
But nobody asks me if I *want* to do it."

Well, Elizabeth got to be five or six,
And she learned to do several other tricks.
Her folks gave a party and Lizzie's mom said,
"Guess what, gang! Our Lizzie can stand on her head!
Now everyone watch our remarkable kid.
Okay, stand on your head, Liz!" And Elizabeth did.
She teetered and tottered and didn't quite fall,
And she wished she could just crawl away from it all.
"It's strange," Lizzie thought. "They just tell me, 'Go to it!'
But nobody asks whether I *want* to do it.
I wonder if they'd think that things were so fine
If they had to do headstands at parties of mine!"

Elizabeth grew to be nine or ten,
And she took up the clarinet and then
When her parents had parties for people they'd met,
After dinner, they'd make Lizzie play clarinet.
Night after night, they'd have Liz entertain
And the truth is, for her, it was less fun than pain.
"It's strange," Lizzie thought. "They just tell me, 'Go to it!'
But nobody asks me if I *want* to do it."
And she said to herself, "Liz, do people like *you*?
Or do they only like all the things you can do?"

Then finally one evening when Liz was fourteen,
Her folks gave a party, the biggest she'd seen.
"All right!" yelled her dad, "May I have your attention?
You will now see a stunt almost too swell to mention.
Our Liz will do something you'll never forget—
She will stand on her head while playing Chopin on her clarinet!"
"On your mark," cried her mother. "Get set, girl, now go!"
The whole room grew quiet. And Lizzie said, ". . . No."
"No?" said her father. "Why what a strange word."
"She means yes," said her mother. "We must have misheard."
"No," replied Lizzie, "you heard what I said.
I will not play Chopin while I stand on my head."

"But why not?" said her mother. "Yes, why?" asked her dad.
Elizabeth's answer was simple and sad.
"It's always seemed strange. You just tell me, 'Go to it!'
But nobody cares whether I *want* to do it.
It makes me feel awful. I wish you'd explain
Why you only seem happy when I entertain.
There are things I can do and things I can be.
I know you like them. But do you like me?"

There was silence till softly her father said, "Oh . . ."
Then, "Oh . . ." said her mother. "We just didn't know."
"We're sorry," her dad said, "and we'll try to change."
"We love you," her mom said, "and it does seem strange
The way that we've always just told you, 'Go to it!'
Without ever asking if you *want* to do it."
So they sent all the party guests off on their way.
And they had a nice dinner . . .
Just the three of them . . .
Talking and listening . . .
And especially listening . . . to what Liz had to say.

I'm Never Afraid

Words and Music by
Sarah Durkee and Christopher Cerf
Illustrated by Hilary Knight

♪ see page 161 for the music

Sometimes I'm afraid of what would happen to me
  if someone came and took me away.
And sometimes I'm afraid of stuff that's on TV,
  or worried if my mom's okay.
And sometimes I'm so scared about the monsters in my closet
  I hardly even dare to blink.
But one thing I can tell you you should never be afraid of
  is sayin' what you really think!

Oh, no, I'm never afraid, I'm never afraid
  to say what's on my mind!
No, I'm never afraid, I'm never afraid
  to say what's on my mind!
There's all kinds of brave
  and all kinds of courageous,
But me I'm the bravest kind,
  'cause I'm never afraid to say what's on my mind!

Well Annie's scared of heights and Dan's afraid of snakes
  and I'm scared to pass the bully next door.
And sometimes I'm afraid they'll make a stupid mistake
  and someone'll start a nuclear war!
But once this kid was braggin' 'bout a brand new bike
  he was plannin' to go out and steal.
I said, "It's *dumb* to do that!" and I wasn't afraid
  'cause I told him how I really feel!

68

(To Say What's on My Mind)

Oh, no, I'm never afraid, I'm never afraid
 to say what's on my mind!
No, I'm never afraid, I'm never afraid
 to say what's on my mind!
There's all kinds of brave
 and all kinds of courageous,
But me I'm the bravest kind,
 'cause I'm never afraid to say what's on my mind!

I know a macho guy who pumps his muscles every day
Who's *ter-ri-fied* of sayin' somethin' wrong!
I know a little boy who says the hardest things to say,
Yeah, *he's the one* who's really big and strong!

My mother's got a friend who likes to hug me a lot,
 yeah, he's nice to me beyond a doubt.
But if somebody hugs me and it bugs me a lot,
 I say "Mom, they've gotta CUT THAT OUT!"
You might be scared the truth is gonna make 'em mad,
 and you're petrified to have a fight,
But come right out and say it and you won't be afraid,
 if you're sayin' what you know is right!

Oh, no, I'm never afraid, I'm never afraid
 to say what's on my mind!
No, I'm never afraid, I'm never afraid
 to say what's on my mind!
There's all kinds of brave
 and all kinds of courageous,
But me I'm the bravest kind,
 'cause I'm never afraid to say what's on my mind!

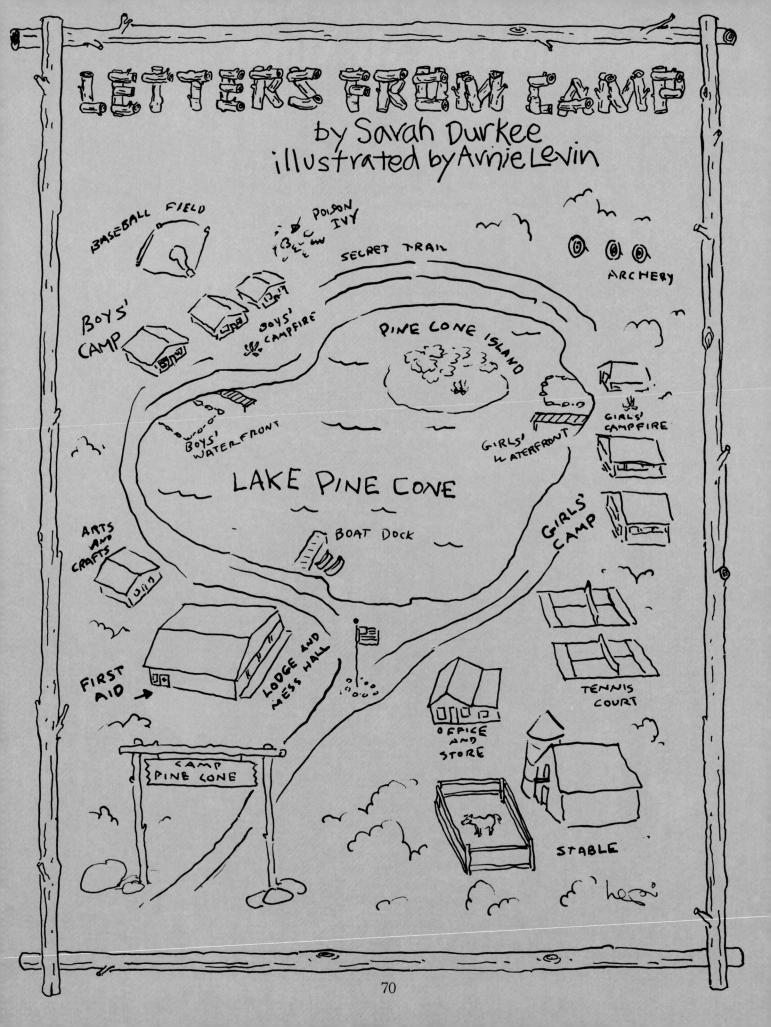

Dear Dad,   June 29

I'm writing you because Beth the counselor says that's what we have to use this half hour for. After this I have swimming. I hope we don't have to do the crawl stroke because remember at the Y last year I kept swimming crooked into the ropes? It's okay here but I would still rather be home with Mom even though you and Mom say camp will be the best time of my life. You also said I would love Girl Scouts and it was dumb except when we learned what to do when somebody catches on fire.

Anyway what I want to know is was it ~~your new wife~~ her idea to sneak fuzzy pajamas with a tail into my knapsack right where everybody can see them?? for her information I am NINE YEARS OLD!! My bunkmate's name is Liza and she says that's exactly the kind of stupid thing her stepmother does. Well that's all. Write me if you want (just you though.)

              Love,

              Nikki

                              July 6

Dear Dad,

Well here I am again before swimming. Guess what? I did the crawl stroke right! I like it a little better here now. We built an Indian Totem Pole.
    Thanks for the letter that was really funny about the car windows being open in the carwash!! I wish I had been there oh well. Were her kids there? Thanks for the cookies. By the way did you make them or did ~~Stephanie your new wife~~ Stephanie? Mom sent me brownies and comics. I am going to ask Liza to come and visit sometime when camp is over. (To Mom's house.)
    Well that's all for now.

              Love,

              Nikki

July 17

Dear Dad,

Hello it's me again. Guess what? I got my minnow badge in swimming!!!! I'm the youngest one to get it. Liza is still Starfish because she has an Ear Infection. Plus somebody said there's bloodsuckers in the lake so she says no way is she going in far. She wears a T-shirt in and her high-top sneakers. By the way thanks for the letter I didn't know ~~she~~ Stephanie used to be a swimming coach I thought she was only a life guard. I'm having a REALLY good time here now my counselor Beth is really nice. She's a really great swim teacher tell Stephanie so I don't need Stephanie to coach me if I come to visit, thanks. I made Mom a belt buckle out of shells. I made you a glasses case out of cardboard and fish bones. The smell will go away when it dries more I think.

Love
Nikki

P.S. Parents weekend is next week remember.
Mom is coming at 10:00 Saturday morning so
will you come then too? Liza's stepmother
isn't coming so I told her mine wasn't either.
okay?
P.S.S. I miss you.

WELCOME
PARENTS

July 23

Dear Dad,

If you bring Stephanie I'll KILL you!!!! It's not fair that she's coming I don't care if you and Mom think it's okay. And I don't care if you and her stay at the motor lodge and not here it still means she's coming!!! I hate it here now anyway so don't even bother coming at all okay? Liza's father isn't coming either so big deal if mine doesn't I'll just say I don't have a father.

Nikki

Dear Dad,

July 28

I'm really glad just you came to parents weekend for a little while. I hope Stephanie didn't feel too bad about me not wanting her to come. Thanks again for the speedo bathing suit it fits. Mom said she bet Stephanie picked it out because <u>you</u> sure don't have any taste in clothes! Ha ha just kidding!

Liza thinks you're neat. Maybe when camp is over she could visit me at your house. Well only three more days here I can't believe it! My unit is cooking pigs-in-Blankets for the whole camp tonight. I'll make them for you when I get ~~to be~~ back sometime.

Well that's all.

Love,
Nikki

P.S. Does Stephanie know how to do the Butterfly stroke? That's all I need to do to get my Tuna badge next summer. I don't want her to teach me I was just wondering.

CAMP PINE CONE

Dear Dad,

August 5

Hi again! It sure is great to be back home. That was a pretty fun trip back we all had wasn't it.

I was really mad at first that Stephanie came but it was okay. I'm sorry Liza got carsick though I hope the seats aren't wrecked. Stephanie was ~~really~~ nice about it. Liza said her stepmother is a gross pig compared to Stephanie. I guess some stepmothers are ~~worse~~ better than others.

Anyway thanks for the ride and everything. I'll see you next month. (Her kids DEFINITELY WON'T BE THERE then, right?)

Love,
Nikki

P.S. I got on the swim team at the Y!! I kept my fingers tight together just like Stephanie said (But I probably would've made the team anyway.) Maybe you can bring her to a meet sometime. If she wants.

P.S.S. Mom says hi.

P.S.S.S. Say hi to Stephanie.

Two Can Play the Same Game

by Mavis Jukes
Illustrated by Pierre Le-Tan

Maria was holding a rubber pig wrapped up in a dish towel.

"What have you got there?" said her grandfather.

"An alive pig," said Maria. She slyly reached inside the towel and squeezed the squeaker.

The pig oinked.

Her grandfather put his crossword puzzle and his pencil on the coffee table. "Well, let's have a look," he said.

Maria walked over. Her grandfather lifted a corner of the towel and slowly shook his head, and whistled. "That's one nice-looking hog," he said to Maria.

"Thank you," said Maria.

Her grandfather's stomach growled. "But I'll tell you something—he's hungry."

Maria stared at the pig.

"Give him to me—I'll hold him," said her grandfather. "And you go warm him up a tortilla and throw in some of that cold chicken in the refrigerator."

"And that leftover guacamole!" he added, as Maria left the room.

Maria warmed a tortilla, rolled up some chicken and guacamole inside it, and brought it into the living room.

"Where's the milk?" said her grandfather.

"WHAT milk?" said Maria.

"Didn't I say this pig needs milk?"

"No," said Maria. "Nobody said anything about milk."

"The pig needs milk," said her grandfather.

Maria loudly sighed. She went into the kitchen and poured milk into a red plastic cup.

When she returned, the tortilla was gone.

"Boy," said her grandfather, wiping his moustache. "That was one hungry pig."

Maria said nothing. She put the cup of milk on the coffee table.

"No pig should ever get that hungry. Or this cold!" said her grandfather. "Feel this hoof. Feel it!"

Maria felt the pig's hoof.

"The pig is fine," she said.

"Fine?" said her grandfather. "FINE? This pig's so cold it makes me cold to look at him."

"The pig is not cold," said Maria. "The pig is wrapped up in a blanket."

"The pig is wrapped up in a dish towel," said her grandfather. He held the pig closer to his chest. *Pobrecito,*" he said in a soft voice. "Poor little thing."

Maria stormed out of the room. She returned, dragging a striped blanket with fringe on the ends. She picked up the plastic cup and peered into it; it was empty.

"Very thirsty, that pig," said Maria's grandfather, taking the blanket from Maria and pulling it over his knees.

Maria stared at her grandfather as he cradled the pig on one arm and drew the blanket up under its snout.

He bent his head over the pig. "Hey, little *bandido,*" he said in a sweet voice. "Is your belly full?" He tickled the top of the pig's head and gave the pig a kiss.

Maria frowned at the pig.

"Yes," said her grandfather. "I've got to congratulate you, Maria. You've got yourself one handsome animal, and I should know. You know how many pigs I've raised in my day?"

"No," said Maria.

"Many pigs. And I'll tell you something: a pig is a very sensitive and intelligent animal. I knew a pig that could smoke a pipe."

"You did not," said Maria.

"Oh, yes I did!" said her grandfather. "The pig could smoke a pipe and watch TV. Of course, not everybody can teach a pig to smoke a pipe—and not every pig can learn. But, hand me my pipe, will you?" he said to Maria. "And my tobacco. I'll see what I can do. And turn on the TV, while you're up."

Maria tromped across the rug and turned on the TV and brought her grandfather his pipe and tobacco.

He handed her the pig. "See if he'll watch TV while I get this ready," he said.

Maria sat down beside her grandfather on the arm of his chair while he packed his pipe. She unwrapped the pig and let it stand on her lap.

She watched cowboys galloping across the screen, watched cowboys drink whiskey and argue about a poker game. "The pig doesn't want cowboys," said Maria. "The pig wants *Wild World of Animals.*"

Her grandfather sighed. "But this is John Wayne!"

"I can't help that," said Maria. "The pig is very intelligent—he wants *Wild World of Animals.*"

Her grandfather looked over at her.

"He does!" said Maria.

"I just got comfortable," said her grandfather.

Maria said nothing. She stared at the screen. Now the cowboys were sitting around a campfire. Suddenly she covered the pig's eyes with her hand. "Don't look!" she cried.

She turned to her grandfather. "They're frying bacon!" she whispered. "He's very sensitive! Change the channel!"

With a grunt, Maria's grandfather got up and slowly walked across the room. He stood in front of the TV for a moment, before turning the knob.

Maria quickly slid from the arm of the chair onto the cushion and kicked off her shoes and covered herself and the pig with the blanket.

"And the pig wants popcorn," said Maria.

A Father Like That

by Charlotte Zolotow
Illustrated by Petra Mathers

I wish I had a father.
But my father went away
before I was born.
I say to my mother,
You know what he'd be like?
"What?" she says.

If he were here,
we'd leave the house together every day.

We'd walk to the corner
together.
And he'd go left to work.
And I'd go right to school.
So long, old man,
till tonight, he'd say.

When he'd come home at night, I'd meet him at the door.
He'd put his arm around me and say,
We made another day, the two of us,
and we'd both laugh.

He'd make a drink for you and a drink for him,
and he'd make you sit down
with him before dinner.

After dinner, we'd all do the dishes together
instead of just you and me,
and I'd do my homework.
When I got stuck, he'd show me how.

And pretty soon he'd say,
Hurry up so we can play
a game of checkers before bedtime.

But at bedtime
he'd say to you,
Oh, just one more.

When I'd be sick in bed,
he'd bring me home a new book
and tell you to lie down
while he sat with me and cheered me up.

He'd bring home good jokes from the office
and say, Hey, old fellow,
have you heard this?
And I'd tell it to all the kids the next day.

He'd rather go down to the store
and have a Coke with me
than sit around having beer
with some other fathers.
He'd never call me sissy if I cried.
He'd just say, Never mind, old fellow,
you'll feel better later on.

He would come in the night
when I had nightmares
and talk to me.

He'd never show off about what a good father he was
at parent-teacher meetings.
And if Miss Barton told him I talk in class,
he'd say, Why sure, all boys do.

And no matter what happened,
he'd be on my side when things went wrong,
even if sometimes he had to say
it was really my fault.

When something bad happened,
I could always
talk to him.

His voice would be very low,
and when he was angry,
He would speak slowly and be kind.

He'd know all my friends by name
and ask something sensible like,
How's your dog?

He'd never joke about me to my friends
or say, Break it up, boys,
to send them home.

He'd understand why
I don't want to wear
that green shirt,
and he'd say to you,
You never were a boy.
You don't know.

He would wrestle with me, and when I wanted
he wouldn't mind if I pounced him a bit.
We'd listen to the doubleheaders together on TV.
When you'd say, Turn it down,
He'd smile and say,
If we make it lower, we won't hear.

And all the while
I'm telling this to my mother,
she is sewing very fast.
"I'll tell you what,"
she says, when I stop talking,
"I like the kind of father
you're talking about.
And in case he never comes,
just remember

when you grow up,
you can be
a father like that yourself!"

The Day Dad Made Toast

by Sarah Durkee
Illustrated by Richard McNeel

I'll never forget the day Dad made toast. It was a sunny Saturday morning in late October near Halloween. I remember it was Halloween because Mom was outside putting a scarecrow with a pumpkin head up on the roof. Dad was in bed.

"Hey kids!" he hollered from their bedroom. "C'mere!"

My older sister Lucy and little brother Danny and I were busy watching the Three Stooges, but we ran upstairs during the commercial. Dad sprang out of bed in his underwear like a ringmaster.

"Here they are!" he bellowed joyfully. "My *kids!!* The greatest kids in the *world!*" He grabbed us to his chest and squished our faces together. This wasn't at all like him. Something was up. "Where's your beautiful mother?!"

"Out on the roof," Lucy said.

He pulled us over to the window that looked out onto the roof. My mom was out there in her ripped overalls with a bunch of tools sticking out of her pockets. She had finished setting up the pumpkin man and was now fixing the TV antenna. Dad tapped on the window.

"LINDA!" he shouted. "COME ON IN, HONEY!"

Mom looked up cheerfully. She had nails in her mouth.

"JUSHT A SHECUND!" she yelled. "I SHEE A LOOSH SHINGLE!"

Clutching her hammer, she scrambled toward the shingle on all fours.

Dad grinned down at us.

"Should I tell her?" he asked.

Mom's hammering rang through the house.

"Tell her *what??* What's going *on??*"

"Well . . ." Dad smiled, and then he broke the big news. "I'M GOING TO MAKE TOAST!!"

"WOW!" we cried. "*Really,* Dad?? *Today??*"

"Yup!" he beamed proudly. "Right this minute! And we're not talking ordinary ho-hum *toast,* believe you me . . . we're talking dad's special *cinnamon* toast!! And I don't want your mom to lift a *finger,* I'm handling the *whole thing!*"

"Oooooh!"

He tapped on the window again. "LINDA!" he yelled. "MEET US IN THE KITCHEN! I HAVE A SURPRISE FOR YOU!"

"OKAY, SWEETHEART!" Mom shouted as she hung from a ladder, clearing leaves from the gutter. "I'LL BE RIGHT DOWN!"

Lucy and Danny and I sat on the end of the bed, waiting for further instructions. We love it when he gets in these moods. One time he decided we should cook Thanksgiving dinner on the outdoor grill. It tasted weird. Another time he decided the whole family was getting flabby, and we started doing calisthenics out in the yard every morning. On the third day he twisted his ankle, so we stopped.

Dad went over to the chair where he always throws his clothes at night and pulled on his jeans. "Okay, kids, listen up!" he said. "Your mother and I both work really hard all week. I figure the least I can do . . ."

Mom started hammering something again.

"I FIGURE THE LEAST I CAN DO," he shouted over the banging, "IS TAKE SOME OF THE HOUSEWORK LOAD OFF HER ONCE IN A WHILE! WE'VE ALL GOT TO LEND A HAND! PITCH IN! DO OUR BIT! SHE'LL REALLY APPRECIATE IT!"

The hammering stopped. Dad pulled on a T-shirt that says "Are we having fun yet?" and jabbed his fist in the air like a football coach.

"Let's hit that kitchen, team!"

We raced him downstairs.

The kitchen was still pretty neat from the night before. We all kind of wandered around for a second not quite knowing how to start. Dad opened and closed a few cabinets. "Now let's see . . ." he muttered. "*Plates. . . .* Where do we keep the ones I like . . . y'know those big blue plates we have? . . ."

Mom knocked on the kitchen door with her elbow. She was lugging two pots of geraniums. Dad flung open the door and gave her a kiss.

"Thanks!" Mom said as she passed through to the living room. "It's about time I brought these indoors!"

Dad sort of jogged along behind her to the doorway. "Breakfast is coming right up, angelface! I'm making my special *cinnamon* toast! Just leave everything to me! You're gonna *love* it!"

Mom's voice drifted back from the family room. "Terrific, hon!"

"Um . . . Linda?" he called. "Where are the big blue plates?"

"In the dishwasher!" Mom yelled.

Dad snapped his fingers. "RIGHT!"

Danny and I got the plates and juice glasses from the dishwasher and started to put them on the table. Mom came back in dragging the vacuum cleaner behind her. She picked up the phone and called her office.

"No, no, kids!" said Dad. "The plates have to be *preheated!* That's what they do in fancy restaurants. It makes the toast stay warm longer!" He grabbed the plates, put them in the oven, and turned away.

"Oh," we said. We turned the oven on. Dad's very absent-minded.

"Hi, it's me," Mom said on the phone. "I spoke to the Blums and they're willing to go to seventy-three-five. They'd like to pass papers on Thursday."

Mom's a real estate agent. They all talk like that.

She hung up the phone, plugged in the vacuum, and rounded the corner to the dining room accompanied by a whir so deafening that we all had to shout.

"OKAY," Dad yelled, "LET'S GET THIS SHOW ON THE ROAD! JENNY,"—that's me—"WE NEED ABOUT A DOZEN SLICES OF BREAD! *WHITE* BREAD, NOT THE HEALTHY KIND."

"BUT MOM LIKES US TO USE THE HEALTHY KIND!" I reminded him.

"JUST THIS *ONCE!* THIS IS 'DAD'S SPECIAL TOAST'! HEALTHY BREAD DOESN'T WORK! NOW WHERE'S THAT DARN TOASTER?!"

"HERE, DAD!" Danny giggled. It had a quilted toaster cover over it.

"WHY WOULD ANYBODY WANT TO COVER UP A TOASTER?!" Dad grumbled.

Lucy and I tried not to laugh but Danny was too young to know any better.

"DADDY COULDN'T FIND THE *TOASTER!*" he shrieked. "HEEE HEE HEE HA HA HA!!"

"I *KNOW* WHERE THE *TOASTER* IS, DANNY, I JUST COULDN'T *SEE* IT! NOW GET OVER THERE AND HELP JENNY COUNT THE BREAD."

The vacuuming stopped. Mom walked through on her way down to the laundry room with a huge armload of dirty clothes.

"Uh, Linda?" Dad said brightly with his head in a cupboard. "Sugar?"

"Yes, cupcake?" she answered.

"No, honey, I mean *where's the sugar,*" said Dad. "I don't see it in here."

"Bottom shelf!" yelled Mom on her way to the basement.

"RIGHT!" yelled Dad, spotting the sugar bag. "Okay, kids! Start toasting that bread! Lucy, you and I will make the cinnamon mixture. Let's see . . . cinnamon . . . sugar . . ."

"How about a bowl to mix it in?" said Lucy, handing him a bowl.

"RIGHT!" said Dad. "Now watch closely." He started spooning sugar and shaking cinnamon. "*Equal parts* of each. That's the real secret to this. A lot of people skimp on the cinnamon."

Mom started a buzz saw in the basement. She's been building new shelves for the family room. Also a sun deck. Also an addition to the garage.

"How's that first batch of toast coming, guys?" Dad called to Danny and me.

"Okay," I said. "What should we do when it's done?"

Mom came up from the basement tugging a bag of cement mix. "Bulkhead's stuck shut," she said. "I better go out and pry it open."

"Butter it and bring it over to me and Lucy *fast,*" Dad said. "We'll sprinkle it with the cinnamon mixture and then whisk each batch into the oven with the preheated plates."

Mom muscled the cement mix out the kitchen door.

"There's orange juice in the fridge," she called over her shoulder.

"Don't you budge, sweetie!" Dad called after her. "I'll take care of it!"

Danny poured the juice and put napkins on the table. I kept buttering the toast when it popped up and IMMEDIATELY brought it to Dad who IMMEDIATELY sprinkled it with the cinnamon mixture and gave it to Lucy who IMMEDIATELY put it in the oven with the preheated plates. Once we'd gotten our system down pat, Dad relaxed a little.

"Y'know, kids," he mused, "times have really changed. I mean *my* father wouldn't have been caught *dead* doing any housework. It just wasn't something men *did;* it was women's work. But we're modern families now, and here you have a manly guy like me pitching in like this after a hard week's work—making breakfast so his wife can take a little break. It's beautiful, isn't it?"

"It's beautiful, Dad."

"We've really come a long way," he said.

"We really have, Dad."

Just as Lucy was putting the last piece of toast in the oven, Mom knocked on the door with her elbow again. "COULD SOMEBODY OPEN THE DOOR, PLEASE?"

Dad rushed over to let her in.

"Thanks. My hands are *filthy*! I didn't even want to touch the doorknob!"

"Ready for the most delicious toast you've ever had in your life, Linda?!" said Dad. We all gathered around the oven.

"Can I wash my hands first?" said Mom. "Or is the flavor peaking this very *second*?"

"Linda, this is no time for sarcasm. Just wash your hands and sit down and relax," said Dad, "and I'll serve you! You too, kids."

Mom washed her hands at the sink, and Lucy, Danny, and I sat down at the table.

"I poured the juice," said Danny.

"You did a great job," Mom smiled as she joined us. "No spills."

"O-kee do-kee!" sang Dad as he opened the oven and brought out the plates. "Hot plates for everybody! Dad's special method!"

He set one in front of each of us.

"Thanks, honey," Mom said.

"Thanks, Dad!!" we all chimed. It did feel like a special occasion. A party, almost, the way he did it.

"And now . . . the *pièce de résistance*! My crowning achievement! The main event! Ladies and gentlemen . . . DAD'S SPECIAL TOAST!!!"

He set the big plate of warm, crispy, buttery cinnamon toast in the center of the table.

"YAAAAAAAY!!" we all cheered. "Hooray for Daaaaaad!!" we applauded.

Dad took a bow and sat down to eat.

Everybody took a couple of pieces of toast and started ooohing and ahhing like mad.

"UNBELIEVABLE!" said Lucy. "The best I've ever had! By far!"

"FRIGHTENINGLY good," said Mom. "Beyond toast. Indescribably delicious."

"Extraterrestrial," I said. "Yummy in the tummy."

We all munched in silence for a minute.

Then Danny spoke up.

"What's the big deal?" said Danny. "All he did was make toast."

"Danny!" Lucy scolded. "That's not very nice! It's really *great* toast!"

"*Perfect* toast!" I cried.

"*Warm* toast!" Mom added.

We all went back to munching.

"But Mom does a million times more housework every *day,* and we hardly even thank her at all! And we NEVER go 'Yaaaay.'"

We all looked at Danny.

Then we looked at Mom.

Everybody was quiet.

Then Dad took a deep breath.

He started yelling "YAAAAAAAY!" at the top of his lungs, and then so did Lucy and Danny and I, and we made Mom get up and take a bow.

"Thank you!" she laughed, pretending she was holding a microphone. "You're a beautiful audience! It's a pleasure to be here!"

We whistled and hollered and clapped and stamped our feet.

Mom blew a kiss like a movie star and raised her glass of orange juice.

"A toast!" she declared.

"A toast!" said Lucy, lifting her glass.

"A toast!" said Dad, holding up a piece of toast.

"To my perfect, helpful children," said Mom.

"Yeah!" we said.

"To my loving, supportive husband," said Mom.

"Hear, hear!" Dad said.

"To the yard!" said Mom. She put down her glass and grinned.

"Huh?" we said.

"To the *yard*," Mom repeated, gesturing toward the pile of cement bags. "What do you say we go work off some of that hearty breakfast?"

She headed for the door, then turned and winked. "Oh, and by the way . . . what are you guys making for dinner?"

(P.S. . . . We went out for pizza.)

The Stupid Song

Words and Music by Robin Batteau
Illustrated by Gary Zamchick

♪ see page 162 for the music

BROTHER

Everything's so stupid, stupid, stupid, stupid, stupid, stupid, stupid,
And I hate it, hate it, hate it, hate it, hate it, hate it,
Maybe if I say it, say it, say it, say it, say it to myself,
I won't have to yell at my mom.

Bein' a kid is no bowl of cherries,
No bed of roses,
No piece of cake.
When I act like a grown-up,
They say I'm precocious.
When I act like a kid,
They tell me that I'm hopeless.

SISTER

Everything's so stupid, stupid, stupid, stupid, stupid, stupid, stupid,
And I hate it, hate it, hate it, hate it, hate it, hate it,
Maybe if I say it, say it, say it, say it, say it to myself,
I won't have to yell at my dad.

Bein' a kid is no laughing matter,
No silver platter,
No yellow brick road.
When I say what I think,
They say, "Kid, you're too young."
And then when I'm quiet,
They say, "Cat got your tongue?"

MOM AND DAD (in unison)
Everything's so stupid, stupid, stupid, stupid, stupid, stupid, stupid,
And we hate it, hate it, hate it, hate it, hate it, hate it,
Maybe if we say it, say it, say it, say it, say it to ourselves,
We won't have to yell at our kids.

Bein' a grown-up's no spring picnic,
No day at the beach,
No easy street.
Even if you're makin'
    their favorite treat,
You can lead your kids to lunch
But you can't make 'em eat!

THE FAMILY
Everything's so stupid, stupid, stupid, stupid, stupid, stupid, stupid,
And I hate it, hate, it hate it, hate it, hate it, hate it,
Maybe if I say it, say it, say it, say it, say it to myself,
I won't have to yell at . . . THEM!

Talk It Over

Words and Music by Carly Simon and Jacob Brackman
Illustrated by Martha Perske

♪ see page 163 for the music

MOM: You okay?
DAUGHTER: Sure, I'm okay.
MOM: You look like there's somethin' you might want
    to say.
DAUGHTER: Who me?
   No way!
MOM: Did anything happen at school today?
DAUGHTER: Just the usual—Workin' and playin'.
MOM: Honey, that's not what your face is sayin'.

    You'd be surprised
    How pressures rise
    The more you hide
    Behind your pride—
    Don't keep things bottled up inside.

    We'll both feel better if we talk it over.
    We'll both feel better if we talk.
    We'll both feel better if we talk it over.
    We'll both feel better if we talk.

    Talk it over. . . .

DAUGHTER: Okay, an awful thing happened
    During recess.
    Ms. Draba keeps a pair of china dolphins in
    her desk,
    And I only wanted to show 'em to Stephen,
    But Ms. Draba came in, and she started screamin'.
    She said, "How dare you open my drawer?"
    She didn't even ask what I did it for!
MOM: She yelled at you and hurt your feelings.
DAUGHTER: She must've thought she had caught me
    stealing
    'Cause she called me a "sneak."
MOM: She must've been freaked!
DAUGHTER: Oh yeah . . . she was really, REALLY
    freaked!
MOM: And you must've been too shocked to explain
    you only wanted a peek.
DAUGHTER: Yeah. . . .
MOM: Did you think that I would scold you?
DAUGHTER: Yeah . . . but now I'm glad I told you!

MOM AND DAUGHTER (*together*):
        We'll both feel better if we talk it over.
        We'll both feel better if we talk.
        We'll both feel better if we talk it over.
        We'll both feel better if we talk.

        Talk it over. . . .

PERSKE

DAUGHTER: You all right?

MOM: Sure, I'm all right.

DAUGHTER: You woke up looking a bit of a fright.

MOM: Who me? It's just this awful light.

DAUGHTER: Didn't you meet with your boss
last night?

MOM: That was just a friendly visit.

DAUGHTER: Well, something's wrong. Come on,
what is it?

DAUGHTER:

You'd be surprised
How pressures rise
The more you hide
Behind your pride—
Don't keep things bottled up inside.

We'll both feel better if we talk it over.
We'll both feel better if we talk.
We'll both feel better if we talk it over.
We'll both feel better if we talk.

Talk it over. . . .

MOM: Quit it! I admit it! I really got uptight!
It started out friendly, but it turned into a fight.
When he took me to a restaurant, I knew it
wasn't right.
At first I was ready to bask in his praise,
Ready to thank him and ask for a raise.
But he said, "Costs are up, sales are in a rut . . ."
So would I volunteer to kindly take a cut???

DAUGHTER: But you've worked so hard. . . .
What a payoff!

MOM: He threatened me with a possible layoff!

DAUGHTER: The man's a dweeb, and that's a fact!

MOM (*crying in background*): I swore I wouldn't worry
you . . .

DAUGHTER: You're always so concerned
with how a mom's SUPPOSED to act.

MOM: Yeah . . .

DAUGHTER: Were you scared that I'd be scared?

MOM: Yeah—even though you know I know
We need to share what needs to be shared!

MOM and DAUGHTER (*together*):
We'll all feel better if we talk it over.
We'll all feel better if we talk.
We'll all feel better if we talk it over.
We'll all feel better if we talk.

Talk it over. . . .

From Here to Forever

Words and Music by Kris Kristofferson,
Glen Clark, Stephen Bruton and Billy Swan
Illustrated by Stacey Schuett

♪ see page 166 for the music

FATHER: Think you can get to sleep now, honey?

DAUGHTER: I think so . . . Daddy?

FATHER: Hm?

DAUGHTER: Is tomorrow a home day or an on-the-road day?

FATHER: On-the-road day. But I'll be home before you can say Charleston-to-Charlotte-to-Chattanooga!

DAUGHTER: I wish you didn't have to travel so much. I wish you had a job near home.

FATHER: Yeah, but look at it this way. If I had a job near home, we'd never get a chance to miss each other. And if we never missed each other, we'd never know how good it feels to be together again!

DAUGHTER: I never thought of it that way. . . .

FATHER: I'll call you tomorrow night, honey.

DAUGHTER: G'night, Daddy.

FATHER: Good night, sweetheart.

Cool shadows fall through the moonlight,
Soft as the breeze through your hair,
And the smile on your face while you're sleeping
Is the answer to anyone's prayer.
Fill your heart for the morning tomorrow
'Cause you still got a long way to grow,
And the love that you're dreaming will guide you
And live like a song in your soul!

And, darlin', when we're not together,
There's one thing I want you to know:
I'll love you from here to forever
And be there wherever you go.

There are so many feelings to follow,
So many chances to take,
So many ways you can stumble,
Someday your heart's gonna break.
Darlin', take all the chances you're given,
Do all you know you can do,
And if you need a reason for livin',
Do it for love and for you.

And, darlin', if we're not together
There's one thing I want you to know:
I will love you from here to forever
And be there wherever you go.

Sleep tight, sweetheart. . . .

The Night We Started Dancing

by Ann Cameron
Illustrated by Eve Chwast

I am named after my dad, Luis, but everybody calls me Luisito. I live with my grandfather and grandmother; my four uncles; my two aunts; my cousin, Diego; a girl named Maria who helps my grandmother; our two dogs, Chubby and Pilot; our two cats, Stripes and Hunter; and our big green parrot, Bright Star, that my grandmother always says she is going to bake and serve for dinner someday.

We live in a town called Santa Cruz, in Guatemala, Central America. Santa Cruz has a park where there are great band concerts, free, every week. It has a public school, and a big college for army cadets, and it has an electronics store where you could special-order a computer, but it doesn't have paved streets, it has only dirt streets that turn to dust in the winter when it's dry, and to mud in the summer when it rains.

I like dirt streets. It goes with the special thing about Santa Cruz, which is that it's a very old town. It was a town before Columbus discovered America, and before the Spaniards came from Spain to steal our land and our gold and make slaves of people, because they said their religion was the true one, and God liked them better than us.

On the edge of Santa Cruz there is a high hill covered with old pine trees and the ruins of pyramids and an ancient fortress. That's where the headquarters of our people was, the headquarters of the kingdom of the Quichés,* where our ancestors fought the Spaniards harder than anybody in Guatemala, before they lost for good.

Once, when I was six, a real Spaniard from Spain came to our house for dinner. He was going to do some business with my grandfather, so my grandmother invited him.

The whole dinner I kept watching my grandfather and the Spaniard all the time, and looking at my grandfather's big machete knife that he keeps by the front door.

Finally, I couldn't stand it. I said, "*Con permiso,* excuse me," and got up from the table and followed my grandmother into the kitchen when she went to get more food, and I even ducked under Bright Star's perch to get there faster.

*(pronounced kee-CHAYS)

"When?" I asked my grandmother. "When is he going to do it?"

"Who?" my grandmother said. "Do what?"

"When is Grandpa going to kill the Spaniard?" I whispered, and Bright Star hissed in his loudest voice, "Kill the Spaniard!" and the Spaniard looked around fast and dropped his fork.

My grandfather stopped munching his tortilla. "Don't be concerned," he said to the Spaniard, "we just have a crazy parrot," and my grandmother said, "One day I am going to bake you, Bright Star!"

Then she took me into one of the bedrooms and closed the door.

"What is this all about?" she said. "Why would Grandpa kill the Spaniard?"

"For being a Spaniard," I said.

"Are you crazy?" my grandmother said. "How can the Spaniard help being a Spaniard? He was born one, just like you were born a Guatemalan and a Quiché. Don't you know the battles with the Spaniards were over hundreds of years ago? We have to judge people by what they do, not by where they come from. And we have to fight our own battles, too, not the ones our ancestors fought."

So that was when I first found out that we'd never get our kingdom back—at least not the way it used to be.

My grandfather was born poor, and he never went to school. He worked from the time he was six years old, out in the wheat fields and the cornfields, hoeing. Every day when he finished work and went home, he would pass by his own dad in the street, drinking and spending all the family money. My great-granddad never helped my granddad at all. But my granddad just kept working, and when he was twenty, he started buying land—pieces nobody thought were good for anything—and on the land he planted apple orchards, and when the apples grew all over, big and beautiful, he got rich. He built a big house for my grandmother and our family, with five big bedrooms, and a patio in the middle full of flowers, and a living room where he and my grandmother put up all the pictures of both their families, except my grandfather never put up a picture of his dad. Then, last year, he must have finally started feeling sorry for his father, because he got his picture out of a drawer, and dusted it off, and put it up in the living room, only not with the rest of the pictures. So now my great-grandfather is staring out at the rest of the family, kind of ashamed-looking, from behind a fern.

My grandmother only learned to read four years ago, but she made my aunts and uncles study hard in school, and now she's making me do it, too. When I asked her why I had to study so hard, she said, "So that you aren't working with a hoe in the fields all your life, with the sun beating down on your head like a hammer."

When my grandparents' kids got to be old enough to study in the capital, my grandparents bought a house there for them to live in. So most of the year my aunts and uncles are there, studying architecture, and economics, and dentistry, and law, and accounting, and psychology. Only my youngest aunt, Celia, who is sixteen, is still living in Santa Cruz all the time. But next year she's going to the capital, too. She says she's going to study to be a doctor. My grandparents are very proud of all their children. The sad thing is, their oldest son, the only one who was studying agriculture and who loved the land the way my grandfather does, was my father, and he died. My mother died with him.

My mother was teaching grade school and my dad was in the last year of his agriculture studies when they died. I was four years old.

It happened four years ago, when my mom and dad and I and Uncle Ricardo were taking a bus from the capital to go back to my grandparents' house for Christmas. The bus terminal was full of dust and people trying to sell ice cream and coconuts and last-minute Christmas presents. Lots of people were going back to their hometowns for the holidays, and there weren't enough buses. Everybody was pushing and shoving to get on the ones there were.

My mom had a suitcase, and my dad had me on his back because he figured I couldn't run fast enough, and Uncle Ricardo was staring toward the sun with his hand shading his eyes, trying to see the bus that goes to Santa Cruz.

"Santa Cruz! That's it! Run!" he shouted, and my mom and dad raced for the front door of the bus, and Uncle Ricardo raced for the back, and they did flying dives over the top of a bunch of other people. My mom and dad got seats right behind the driver, and I sat on my mom's lap. Uncle Ricardo got stuck at the back, standing up.

Everybody pushed the windows down to get more air, and the driver put the bus in gear, but it didn't move, and his helper, the ticket taker, got out a hammer and a wrench and raised the hood on the bus and hammered on something for a while, and then the driver tried to move the bus again, and it went, and Uncle Ricardo heard my mother say, "A miracle! What a miraculous miracle!" and the ticket taker ran after the moving bus and jumped in the open door with the hammer and the wrench in his hand, and we were off.

Uncle Ricardo settled in and tried to take his elbow out of the stomach of the person on his right, and get his feet out from under the feet of the person on his left. My mom and dad were probably about the only ones who could see out the window, and who knew how the driver was driving.

The bus didn't go very fast, because it couldn't with so many people on it, but after a while Uncle Ricardo felt the bus lurch, and he heard my dad say to the driver, "Be careful, brother!" so he figured that the bus driver must have been taking a chance passing on a mountain curve.

A little while later he felt the bus twist again, and he heard my father say to the driver, "A man who foresees trouble and prevents it, is worth two men." But it seemed like the driver didn't feel like listening, because a little while later Uncle Ricardo heard my father say, "No matter where you are going, you don't have to get there first. The thing is, to get there."

And after that he heard my mother say, "Driver, there is more time than life."

And that was all he heard, except for my mother's voice just once more, shouting, "Luisito!" just before my father grabbed me with one hand and threw me out the window.

The bus driver went head-on into another bus. And my mother was right, because time just keeps going on and on and on, but she and my dad and the bus driver and the ticket taker and a lot of other people ran out of life completely.

Uncle Ricardo was okay because he was at the back, and I was okay.

The only part I remember begins with the grip of my father's hand, and how it hurt when he shoved me through the window frame. But I don't like to remember. I like to think about daytime things, my aunts and uncles, and things that are happening now.

But sometimes I still dream about it, being thrown out the window. In the dream I am little again, the same age I was then, and I land down a hillside in a freshly hoed field, just the way I really landed, but it is not daytime, it is almost completely dark, and I get up and go back to the wrecked bus, to find my mom and dad, but it gets darker and darker, and I never can find them.

Uncle Ricardo says one day I won't have the dream anymore. He says that my parents loved me a lot, and that I will always have them in my heart. He says one day my dream self will understand that, too. It will know that my parents are always with me when I remember them. It won't have to go back to the wrecked bus to look for them anymore.

And really I am okay, and Uncle Ricardo is okay, and my grandmother also is okay, because she loves all her children very much, but equally. The only one who has not been okay is my grandfather, because he loved my dad more than anybody. My dad wasn't only his son, he was his best friend.

The first Christmas after the accident we didn't celebrate, because nobody wanted to. But the next Christmas we didn't celebrate either, because Grandpa didn't want to. On the anniversary of the accident, he cut a lot of white roses and put them in front of my parents' wedding picture that hangs in the living room, and we visited their graves at the cemetery, so that was all there was of Christmas that year, too.

And from the beginning my grandmother said we shouldn't mention my mom and dad in front of my grandfather because it might upset him too much. She said we should just wait, and in time he would get better.

But it got to be September of the third year after my father died, and my grandfather still wasn't any better. My aunt Patricia, who had been leaving my cousin Diego with us a lot in Santa Cruz, decided to take Diego to the city. She said it was because she didn't have so many courses and she would have more time to spend with him, but Uncle Ricardo told me it was really because she thought it was too gloomy for Diego around our house.

The only reason I liked being in the house is that I like my grandmother and Celia a lot, my grandmother because she never yells at anybody, and Celia because she treats me like a grown-up. She got me to help her with a lot of projects, especially her Laugh Development Project, in which she said she needed the opinion of a man.

She wanted to develop four new laughs, even though my grandmother said it was a waste of time, and she couldn't see what was wrong with the laugh Celia was born with.

Celia said these are modern times, and a person should have five of everything. She said her original laugh was for when she really felt like laughing, and the other four would be for when she couldn't afford to be serious. She wanted my opinion because she wanted to make sure the four new laughs would be good enough to impress boyfriends.

So when Grandpa wasn't around, she practiced in front of the big cracked mirror on the patio.

"Hah, hah, HAH, HAH, hah," went the first laugh, which is a rapid one where she tosses her long black hair back behind her shoulders. That is her Rio de Janeiro laugh.

"Ho ho ho," she laughs slowly, and rubs her chin thoughtfully with the finger of one hand. That's her Paris laugh.

"Hee hee hee," she giggles, and covers her eyes with her hands. That's her Tahiti laugh.

"Hoo, hoo, hoo, hoo," she laughs, and raises her eyebrows very high. That's her Mexico City laugh.

She got all the ideas for the laughs from TV and from fashion magazines. After she got them all worked out, I told her they were all good, except the Tahiti laugh, which looked like she was just waking up in the morning, so she decided to rename it a waking-up laugh, to throw a stretch into it.

So she did. But just when she had them all perfect, Bright Star got them perfect, too. He sang them all off in a row, and then he said, in my voice, "Laugh Development Project."

"Now I can't bring any boyfriend home!" Celia said. "Either I can't bring one home, or I can't use my laughs."

"Not only that," I said, "Grandpa is going to know about this for sure."

Celia shrugged. "Maybe he'll borrow a laugh," she said. "He doesn't seem to have one of his own. Anyway, what more can he do? We already don't have Christmas anymore."

Sure enough, when Grandpa came home, Bright Star talked. He laughed all four laughs, and then imitated me, saying "Laugh Development Project."

It happened at dinner. My grandfather looked at Bright Star, and he looked at Celia, and he looked at me, but all he said was, "After school tomorrow, I want to take you out to the orchards, Luisito."

So I said okay, and the next afternoon we hiked out to the orchards.

"You are around your Aunt Celia too much," my grandfather said, but not unkindly. "You need the influence of a man."

"I am a man," I said.

"You are?" my grandfather said. "How do you know?"

"Celia said so."

He looked at me and said it took more than Celia's saying so to make somebody a man, and then he started telling me about the trees, and what you had to do to take care of them, and how many different kinds of apples there were, and how you could tell them apart.

But a bad thing happened, because the orchards are right next to the pyramids and the forts of the old kingdom, and I kept thinking about them and wanting to go over there, instead of listening to my grandfather.

"Luisito," he said suddenly, "how many kinds of apples do I have?"

And I couldn't tell him.

"You're not listening! Your father understood and remembered everything when he was your age!" he shouted. "Go on home to your grandmother!"

So I left, and instead of going straight home, I went over to the pyramids and ran up to the top of the biggest and stood there listening to the branches of the pine trees in the wind. It didn't help anything. And then I walked home alone.

When I told my grandma what happened, she said, "Your dad did understand and remember very well when he was your age. But when he was your age, he also played with matches once and set a whole cornfield on fire. It took us, the neighbors and the whole fire department to put it out."

"Tell Grandpa that!" I said. "Remind him about it!"

"I will sometime," my grandmother said, "but not now."

"When?" I asked. "You said Grandpa would get better and we just had to be patient. He used to make jokes, Celia says. He used to take everybody on trips. Now he never does, and he never gets any better."

"You are right," my grandmother said.

"Besides," I said, "Christmas is coming, and I am tired of not having Christmas, and so is Celia."

"You're probably right," my grandmother said. "We should celebrate Christmas."

And she actually used the telephone, which she never uses, to call up Ricardo and talk to him about it.

And that night at dinner, she told my grandfather, "It's time we started to celebrate Christmas again."

"I would rather not," my grandfather said.

"The children say they won't come home for Christmas, unless we celebrate, like the old days. Luis and Celia say they would rather go into the city to be with Ricardo and everybody if we don't celebrate Christmas."

"Um," my grandfather said.

"I might go, too," my grandmother said.

"*You* might go?" my grandfather said.

"Yes, I probably will go," my grandmother said.

"You would *leave* me?" my grandfather said.

"Just for Christmas," my grandmother said.

"It wouldn't be good," my grandfather said. "We've been together thirty-one years. You've never been away. Not one day!"

"Times change," my grandmother said.

"Well," my grandfather said, "we had better celebrate Christmas. But I won't dance."

"You don't have to dance," my grandmother said. "Nobody has to dance. But at least we will have dance music, anyway."

Celia and I made a beautiful golden Christmas tree out of corn husks that we cut to fasten on wires and make the shape of branches. When we were done, the tree went all the way to the ceiling, and we draped it with red chains of tinsel. And my grandmother stood in front of the stove all Christmas Eve day making the tamales for the midnight dinner—corn stuffed with chicken and meat and olives and raisins and hot chili sauce, and wrapped in banana leaves to cook. And everybody arrived from the city about six-thirty at night, just in time for the supper we were going to have to tide us over to the real dinner at midnight.

Uncle Ricardo brought Diego and me about sixty firecrackers to set off at midnight, when all the kids in town go outside to set off firecrackers, so we were feeling good. And my grandfather had dressed up in his best and happiest clothes, new pants, and a cap that makes him look as young as my uncles.

Everybody hugged, and we all sat down to eat, but nobody talked much until we were almost finished, when Aunt Patricia said, "All the same, it's sad anyway."

And my Uncle Pedro, who had been an exchange student in the U.S. for one year of high school, said, "If the roads had shoulders, the way the highways do in the U.S., they never would have died."

And Celia said, "So in the great U.S.A. there are no traffic accidents?"

And before Pedro could answer her, my grandfather got up out of his chair and went out on the patio, and we all stopped talking.

"Luisito," my grandmother said, "go be with your grandfather."

So I went out on the patio and stood by my grandfather, who was looking up at the sky and wouldn't look down.

I just stood there by him, looking up, too.

There was a full moon, shining down on the patio and on the papery violet leaves of the bougainvillea, and my grandfather spoke, in a choked voice.

"See the leaves? There are so many you can't see the branch, and all different.

"And we are like them, all different, but holding on to an invisible branch—but two of us are missing!

"Why do they have to talk about it? Don't they know I've cried enough? What do they think I do out in the orchard, but cry?"

"You should cry with us," I said, and I saw my grandfather's eyes drop tears, and we stood there a long time.

Everybody else had gone into the living room, and while we were standing there, the dance music started, very slowly, low music, soft like smoke, winding into the moonlight.

"Oh, Luisito," my grandfather said. "What can we do? What can anybody do? Luisito, we should dance."

And so my granddad and I danced, around the cage of Bright Star, who was sleeping under a new Christmas blanket, and past the cracked mirror and the bougainvillea vine, and then, very slowly, into the living room. And then I danced with Celia, and my grandfather put his arms around my grandmother and danced with her, and everybody danced with everybody, straight through until midnight when the fireworks started going off in huge booms all over town, and we all held hands, and everyone of us kissed every other one, and I noticed for the first time in a long time that in the photo of my mom and dad, above Grandpa's white roses, they were smiling.

The Little Boy and the Old Man

by Shel Silverstein

Said the little boy, "Sometimes I drop my spoon."
Said the little old man, "I do that too."
The little boy whispered, "I wet my pants."
"I do that too," laughed the little old man.
Said the little boy, "I often cry."
The old man nodded, "So do I."
"But worst of all," said the boy, "it seems
Grown-ups don't pay attention to me."
And he felt the warmth of a wrinkled old hand.
"I know what you mean," said the little old man.

Twanna and Me

A True Story by Orlando Perez

My daughter Twanna helps me to read, and she is only eight years old. She is very smart in all her work and she reads most of the time. When she teaches me she corrects me when I am wrong. She chooses some of the books from her school, and some from home.

After supper she says, "Okay, Perez, let's read."

The first thing she does is read two or three pages to start me off. Then she says, "Now you go." And she pushes me to read because she wants me to learn.

Twanna is only my stepdaughter and at first we had a rough time to get along. She thought I was taking her mother away from her. But she understands now that her mother needs a husband and she needs a father.

Her mother said, "Twanna, do you want to help Perez to read?"

"Yes, mom, I'll show him," she said. "I'll be his teacher."

Sometimes I tell her, "Now I know how to read."

She says, "No you don't. I'm still your teacher."

When Orlando Perez finished writing this piece, he showed it to Twanna. She was delighted and asked to take it to school, where she read it to her entire class.

106

Like Me

by Emily Kingsley
Illustrated by Martha Perske

I went to my dad and I said to him,
There's a new kid who's come to my school.
He's different from me and he isn't too cool.
No, he's nothing at all like me, like me,
No, he's nothing at all like me.

He runs in a funnyish jerkyish way,
And he never comes first in a race.
Sometimes he forgets which way is first base,
And he's nothing at all like me, like me,
No, he's nothing at all like me.

He studies all day in a separate class,
And they say that it's called "Special Ed."
And sometimes I don't understand what he's said,
And he's nothing at all like me, like me,
No, he's nothing at all like me.

Suggested by *Just Like Me,* a book by Jennifer Fink.

His face looks kind of different from mine,
And his talking is sometimes so slow.
And it makes me feel funny and there's one thing I know;
He is nothing at all like me, like me,
No, he's nothing at all like me!

And my father said, "Son, I want you to think
When you meet someone different and new
That he may seem a little bit strange, it's true,
But he's not very different from you, from you,
No, he's not very different from you.

Well I guess, I admitted, I've looked at his face;
When he's left out of games, he feels bad.
And when other kids tease him, I can see he's so sad.
I guess *that's* not so different from me, from me,
No, that's not very different from me.

And when we're in Music, he sure loves to sing,
And he sings just like me, right out loud.
When he gets his report card, I can tell he feels proud,
And that's not very different from me, from me,
No, that's not very different from me.

And I know in the lunchroom he has lots of fun;
He loves hot dogs and ice cream and fries.
And he hates to eat spinach and that's not a surprise,
'Cause that's not very different from me, from me,
No, that's not very different from me.

And he's always so friendly, he always says hi,
And he waves and he calls out my name.
And he'd like to be friends and get into a game,
Which is not very different from me, from me,
No, I guess that's not different from me.

And his folks really love him. I saw them at school,
I remember on Open School Night—
They were smiling and proud and they hugged him real tight,
And that's not very different from me, from me,
No, that's not very different from me.

So I said to my dad, Hey, you know that new kid?
Well, I've really been thinking a lot.
Some things are different . . . and some things are not . . .
But *mostly* he's really like me, like me,
Yes, my new friend's . . . a lot . . . like me.

The Biggest Problem
(Is in Other People's Minds)

Words and Music by Don Haynie
Illustrated by Simms Taback

♪ see page 167 for the music

My brother Bobby never listens when I talk;
Pays close attention though, and watches like a hawk.
Took some time for my hands to learn the signs,
But now the two of us, we get along just fine.

Bobby's biggest problem is in other people's minds;
We do things we like to do and have a great time.
Some kids stay away, but if they knew him they would find
Bobby's biggest problem really is in other people's minds.

I've known Rosa for a year or so by now;
We've been all around, I sometimes wonder how.
The doors and the stairs give us trouble with her chair;
It may take longer, but we go everywhere.

Rosa's biggest problem is in other people's minds;
We go where we want to go and have a great time.
Since this city's builders didn't think when they designed,
Rosa's biggest problem really is in other people's minds.

Rosa

Angie reads to me the poetry she loves;
Hands brush the pages with the gentleness of doves.
Sings me a song from the piano clear and strong,
She's never seen me, yet she's known me all along.

Angie's biggest problem is in other people's minds;
We go hiking, we go swimming, in the summer sunshine.
Anyone can see I'm lucky she's a friend of mine,
And that Angie's biggest problem is in other people's minds.

Sometimes the biggest problem is in other people's minds;
Be exactly who you are, and you'll do just fine.
Things may look impossible, but try and you will find
That the biggest problem really is in other people's, other people's—
Someday we will change those people's minds!

Cross Your Fingers

by Mavis Jukes
Illustrated by Leo and Diane Dillon

The students at Ridge Elementary Montessori School were sitting on a braided rug, in a circle. Ms. Lee was also seated at the circle—but on a tiny wooden chair, painted red.

"Oh, brother!" said Chuck. "Here we go again."

A small girl with mosquito-bitten legs was standing in the middle of the circle, saying nothing. "So, Hannah," said Ms. Lee, "you have something to share with us?"

Hannah nodded and opened her fist. In her hand were two quartz pebbles. "My teeth," she said. "My bottom two."

"Oh, sure!" said Chuck. Hannah quickly closed her fingers. But Chuck jumped up and pinched her cheeks together and looked into her mouth.

"Sit down!" cried Ms. Lee.

"She didn't lose any teeth," Chuck whispered as he sat down. He looked around at the other children. "What a liar!"

"Those are lovely little stones," said Ms. Lee cheerily. "Thank you, Hannah. Now. Does anyone else have something to share?"

Chuck began waving and straining his arm. Ms. Lee nodded at him. He crawled into the middle of the circle. "I lost another tooth," he announced, with a grin. He opened his mouth as wide as it would go. There were several empty spaces; and in places, big teeth with sawed edges were pushing through his gums. "Here it is . . ." he said. He fumbled in his shirt pocket and pulled out a tooth—yellow, with some blood on the bottom and a silver filling on one side. He held it out in the palm of his hand.

"Ick," said somebody.

Hannah leaned forward to examine the tooth. "The tooth fairy won't give him much for *that* one," she volunteered. "It's not in good condition."

"The tooth fairy?" said Chuck. "Get serious."

Ms. Lee glared at Chuck for a moment. Then she rotated her wrist so she could have a look at her watch. "Who's next? Jesse?"

With difficulty, Jesse arose. He stood, stooped, in the center of the circle—wearing jeans and red high-topped sneakers and a sweatshirt with a silver eagle on the front. Jesse's tight, dark curls poked out from under the hood.

He reached into his sweatshirt and pulled up a key which was attached to a checkered shoelace around his neck. He held it up and hobbled slowly in a circle so that all the children could see it. Some of them looked up only briefly, and then down again at their shoes.

"It's a house key," said Jesse softly.

Ms. Lee made a delighted face. "A house key! Boy! That's a big responsibility for an eight-year-old."

"—for an eight-year-old *wimp*," whispered Chuck.

Ms. Lee looked at him and pointed to the door. And when he had gone to wait in the anteroom, she drummed her fingers on her chest and looked again at Jesse. "What would you like to say about having a house key?"

"Well, it means you can unlock your own door," said Jesse, in a gentle voice, "—and it means you're growing up."

"Right you are," said Ms. Lee.

One of the older girls dumped a house key out of her loafer onto the rug. "I have one, too," she said. Then, a big boy produced one on a key chain and let it swing from the end of his finger.

"Well, aren't we all growing up!" said Ms. Lee. She paused, looking at the faces of the children. "Anyone else with something?" She glanced at the round clock above the door. "Nobody? Then you are all excused, one minute early, to go home."

The children walked out of the schoolhouse—a few balancing books on their heads on the way down the steps. Jesse was the last to gather his things. Ms. Lee had taken Chuck aside near the door and was holding his arm. Jesse passed slowly by them. "Don't spoil things for the little ones," Ms. Lee was saying. "Leave Hannah alone—she likes to pretend."

"Okay," whined Chuck.

"I mean it, Chuck. There are children of different ages here— "

"I know!"

"Well, act like you know! You happen to be almost three years older than Hannah." She lowered her voice. "And don't you ever call Jesse a wimp. Apparently, he has a bum back—so he's more frail than you are. Count your blessings!"

"Can I go now?"

Ms. Lee released Chuck's arm. "But I'm warning you: ANY more baloney from you and I'm going to MARCH RIGHT OVER to the telephone and call your mother. Understand?"

Chuck fixed his shirt and walked away. He elbowed Jesse on his way down the stairs. "Hannah!" he called. "I have news for you. . . ." He slid down the bannister and jumped to the cement. "The tooth fairy is your mom and dad. Really," he said, in a low voice. "I'm not kidding you."

"My mom and dad?" said Hannah.

"Yes!"

She looked thoughtful. "Then where are their tutus? And where are their wings?"

"Where are whose wings?" said Chuck. He threw up his hands. "Don't you get it?"

Hannah stared at him.

"Your mom and dad take the tooth from under your pillow . . ."

"In some cases!" interrupted Jesse, hurrying over. "In some cases, yes!—as you get older. When you're six or seven—or eight—your mom and dad might be the tooth fairy." He gazed at Hannah. "But when you're four or five—now that's a different matter."

Chuck faked a laugh.

Jesse leaned on the bench and put his finger in the air. "Because," he said to Hannah mysteriously, "because when you're still a little kid—still four or five—and you lose a tooth and put it under your pillow, the REAL tooth fairy might flutter from the sky into your room at night . . ."

"Wait JUST a minute!" shouted Chuck. "Who loses teeth when they're four or five? Nobody loses teeth when they're four or five!" he said, with a sneer.

"ALMOST nobody," said Jesse. "But a few kids do. And that makes it all the easier for the tooth fairy—all the more possible! Because, otherwise, think how hard it would be, in the wee hours of the morning, for the tooth fairy to go to EVERY house . . ."

"Go in?" said Chuck. "With the doors locked?" He looked sideways at Hannah. "You believe this wimp?"

"The tooth fairy has keys to fit the locks on every door on earth," said Jesse calmly. His eyes met Hannah's. "Including the door to your house."

"He's lying," said Chuck. "Look at him! He's crossing his fingers behind his back."

"I'm rubbing my back," said Jesse.

"Oh, right," said Chuck.

He turned to Hannah. "How old are you, anyway?"

"I'll be six tomorrow," she told him.

"Well, you're too old to believe in the tooth fairy."

Jesse leaned close to Hannah. "What would he know about the tooth fairy? Look at his teeth!"

"What about my teeth?" said Chuck. He strolled up close to Jesse and put his shoulder as close to Jesse's shoulder as he could without touching him.

"Watch out!" said Hannah. "You'll knock him down!" She put her hand on Jesse's back to steady him and her heart thumped as she felt the hard curve of his spine.

"Need a girl to protect you?" said Chuck to Jesse.

"I might," said Jesse. "And what would be the matter with that? Anyway— you asked about your teeth. And I'll tell you about your teeth: The tooth fairy wouldn't trade a nickel for any tooth in your head. And I'd hate to have to pay your dental bill," said Jesse, as he turned and walked away.

"I'd hate to have to pay your dental bill," repeated Chuck in a high voice. He bent over and limped behind him—then knocked Jesse's books out of his arms and raced away.

Hannah helped Jesse pick up his things. "Want to come over and play?" she asked him.

"Can't."

"Why?"

"I have to rest."

"Your mom says?"

"My back is bugging me," said Jesse. "And I'm pooped! I have to rest."

"Oh," said Hannah quietly. She looked at Jesse. "Could I see your key again?"

Jesse pulled out the shoelace and held it in the air; Hannah watched the key turn and flash in the sunlight. "I'm going to ask my mom and dad for one of those for my birthday tomorrow," she said. "I hope I get one."

"Well," said Jesse. "Cross your fingers."

"There's my mom," said Hannah. "And my brother." Her mother was walking toward them wearing a straw hat and a backpack with a baby boy in it.

"Mom!" Hannah called. "Kenny's eating your hat!"

"He's teething?" said Jesse.

"Yup. His bottom two are coming in—and he's been biting everything. Even my mom!" She ran ahead, then turned and crossed her fingers at Jesse.

He crossed his fingers back.

"Who's that?" said Hannah's mother.

"Jesse. He's a new boy. His back is bent—and today it's bugging him."

"And he's walking home?"

"Yes. And he has his own key to his house."

"Well, he's quite a trooper."

Hannah took her mother's hand. "Mom?"

"What."

"Could I have a key to our house for my birthday? All the kids have them."

"All the kids?"

"All the big kids."

"I'll think about it," said Hannah's mother.

"You always say that," said Hannah.

Later that night, Hannah and her mother sat together on Hannah's bed, looking at a book about bears. Hannah yawned and gazed out the window. The sky was as black as ink; stars were scattered across it like sparks.

"Tired?" said her mother.

"Not really," said Hannah. She slowly blinked. "Did you see that?"

"What."

"Something silver went across the sky! You didn't see it?"

"No."

"You missed it. I think it was a shooting star. Mom?"

"What."

"Are you the tooth fairy?"

"No."

"Chuck says you're the tooth fairy."

"Well, I'm not."

"Is Dad?"

"I certainly hope not. Does he look like the tooth fairy?"

"No. But I'm warning you: You and Dad might turn into the tooth fairy when I'm six."

"Grow wings? By tomorrow? Now I've heard everything."

Hannah tipped her head on her mother's shoulder. "Did you decide about the key yet?"

"Not yet," said her mother.

Hannah closed her eyes. And the next thing she knew—it was morning.

It was morning—sunlight filled her curtains; the air was sweet and warm and she was six. Or was she dreaming? She opened the presents she found at the foot of her bed. She ate birthday waffles with syrup poured from the chimney of a can shaped like a cabin. And her whole family walked her to school.

At lunchtime, she sat with Jesse on a bench in the school yard. Jesse opened a bottle of apple juice. He took a swig and passed Hannah the bottle. Hannah had two swallows and passed it back. "I love apple juice," said Hannah. "Thanks."

She handed Jesse a cupcake. "One each," she said. "My dad made them for my birthday."

"Pretty," said Jesse. He undid the pleated paper. "So you're six," he said, licking the frosting off the top.

"Yup."

"Well, you know, Hannah—sometime soon you might have to say good-bye to the tooth fairy."

He drank and passed the bottle.

Hannah drank and passed it back.

"You're growing up!" continued Jesse. "And you lose something by growing up—but you also get something. Since you're older, you get to do things you couldn't—when you were a shrimp. In a way, you lose the tooth fairy like you lose a tooth. There's an empty spot—then something grows to fill it."

"But where does the tooth fairy go?" said Hannah.

"There are places."

"Where?"

Jesse drank exactly half of what was left in the bottle. He paused, looking for words. "Well, let's just say there are places where the sky is torn. Rips—in the blue, where magic leaks in. That's where the tooth fairy comes from. That's where the tooth fairy goes back to."

Hannah looked down at her cupcake. "So, what you mean is—the magic goes away."

Jesse said nothing.

"I hate Chuck," said Hannah.

She finished her cupcake and tossed the wrapper into the trash. "Did I tell you? I got paints for my birthday. And a stuffed bald eagle with a pink felt tongue . . ."

"Good," said Jesse.

"And a plastic calculator with a turtle on it. And a book about Mother Goose." She stood up. "And this dress with dancing apples on it."

"Nice," said Jesse.

Hannah sat back down. "I didn't get a key, though."

"Oh," said Jesse.

They passed the bottle back and forth, each drinking half until there was just a drop left, then half a drop, then none. They sat without speaking. The wind blew some dried leaves in a circle. It caught and flapped in Hannah's hem, turned up her collar, blew back Jesse's bangs. A cloud covered and uncovered the sun.

Ms. Lee rang a bell at the school door and the children returned to the classroom. She stood up behind her large oak desk and said, "This is a special day for somebody in our class."

Hannah's ears turned red.

"Happy birthday, Hannah! Would you like to tell the class how old you are?"

"I'm six," said Hannah.

Chuck leaned close to Hannah. "Well, you can say good-bye to the tooth fairy," he whispered. "At least according to what Jesse says."

Ms. Lee loudly cleared her throat. "After the sharing circle, we'll sing 'Happy Birthday' to Hannah."

Jesse raised his hand. "May I be first to share? It's about Hannah's birthday . . ."

"Oh, gag!" said Chuck.

Ms. Lee cocked an eyebrow and said to him, "That's IT!" Then, she stood up and straightened her skirt and marched out of the room to call Chuck's mother. She poked her head back in. "You may begin," she said to Jesse.

The children arranged themselves on the rug with Jesse in the center. "What are you staring at?" said Chuck. "I couldn't care less if the teacher calls my mother. Just start! You're not the only one with something to share." He grinned—and the gap in the front of his mouth was one tooth wider.

"I have something to show you," said Jesse.

He pulled his sweatshirt over his head and let it drop, inside out, to the floor. He shook loose his curls; his hair was lit from behind—it fell in tangles on his shoulders. Light winked in the red glass rubies on his belt.

Jesse began to undo the snaps on his shirt.

"Ladies and gentlemen," announced Chuck. "For Hannah's birthday, we'll have a strip tease by Jesse The Wimp!"

Jesse ignored him. He slipped off his shirt, so that his arms and chest were bare.

The room grew very quiet. Jesse turned to lay his shirt on the bookshelf.

"Jesse!" cried Hannah. "What's on your back?"

A gust of wind lifted the curtains. The room darkened.

"Yeah, what's on his back?" somebody whispered. "What's going on?"

Jesse glanced over his shoulder at Hannah; her heart fluttered.

"I don't walk the earth," said Jesse softly, turning to face the children. "I fly." And as he spoke, a shaft of sunlight hit Jesse's body; wings, tightly folded on his back, opened like fans behind him—spilling silver dust into the air. They stood erect, majestic and shimmering; silver feathers cut the sunlight into patterns that swirled in circles on the walls.

Jesse looked at Hannah. "You know who I am," he told her. His eyes glittered like black stars.

Some of the children hid their faces in their hands; others were too stunned to speak or move. "You don't have to be afraid," Jesse told them, in a gentle voice.

Like a dark angel, he kneeled in the dust that lay glimmering on the floor.

"You don't have to be afraid," he said again, and touched somebody's hand. "I'm not the only magic thing you've seen." He looked at the faces of the children. "After all, you live in a world where caterpillars turn into butterflies—where pollywogs swim, grow legs . . . hop away."

Chuck began creeping toward the doorway on his hands and knees. Jesse turned and looked at him.

"Hey, Chuck!" he cried. "How much did you get for that last tooth you lost?" Jesse stood up, reached into his pocket, and pulled out a silver dollar.

"Me?" said Chuck, in a very high voice—pointing to himself.

Jesse stared at him.

"Nothing," said Chuck. Then he brightened a little. "Nothing yet, that is. . . ." He crawled over to Jesse and cautiously put out his hand.

Jesse tossed and caught the silver dollar in the air. And tossed and caught it again, glancing at Chuck's hand. "Did you think this was for *you?*" he said, with a laugh.

He turned to Hannah. "Here," he said. "An advance on your bottom two." And he leaned down and pressed it into her palm. "I have to leave you now," Jesse told her, in a whisper.

Hannah stared at the coin without speaking.

Then, Jesse took off the key and put it around Hannah's neck. "Happy birthday, Hannah. Now, you've got the key; you can open any door. You're six, in a world where an egg can turn into a turtle or an eagle. Or a goose! You're growing up, Hannah, on planet Earth—where flowers change into apples, worms into fireflies! And that kind of magic never goes away."

Hannah covered the key with her hand. And when she looked up, Jesse had climbed onto the windowsill and was carefully guiding his wings through the opening. "Jesse?" she whispered, rising. "Jesse—where are you going?"

"I'm so tired!" said Jesse. "I flew all night last night—did you look out your window? Did you see me? And I flew all night the night before. I have to go now—I have to rest." He turned and slid out of the window on his belly, hanging onto the window sash. His wings began to flap—awkwardly at first, and then in a steadier rhythm.

"Wait!" cried Hannah. Wind from Jesse's wings blew back her hair, blew papers from the bookshelf onto the floor.

"Remember me to your baby brother!" called Jesse. And he reached back in through the space to touch Hannah's cheek good-bye.

With his magnificent wings rippling in the sunlight, with his back arched, and his arms stretched upward in a triumphant gesture, Jesse rose into the air.

"Say good-bye to the tooth fairy!" Hannah cried to the other children.

But before they could reach the window, Jesse flew. And Hannah was the only one who saw him travel upward across the sky—swiftly and silently, like a shooting star—and disappear, like a shooting star, into the blue.

Jimmy Says

Words by David Buskin and Abra Bigham,
Music by David Buskin
Illustrated by Artie Ruiz

♪ see page 158 for the music

BIG BROTHER: Hey, kid, you're lookin' pretty down in the dumps. Tell your big brother about it.

LITTLE BROTHER: Aw, it's just the kids at school. They keep tellin' me what I *should* do, and what I *shouldn't* do, and I'm afraid if I don't listen to them, well, they might not want to be my friends anymore.

BIG BROTHER: Hey, don't worry. There's a guy in my class that used to make *me* feel that way all the time, too. And then one day, I figured out there's another way to go. . . .

Jimmy says, "Do this . . ."
Jimmy says, "Do this . . ."
I say, "I don't want to!"
Jimmy says, "Do this . . ."
Jimmy says, "Do this . . ."
I say, "I don't want to!"

Trying to make up my own mind,
Got my own direction to find!
Yeah, I know Jimmy's cool,
And everyone in school
Usually does what Jimmy does
Without thinking, just because

Jimmy says, "Try this . . ."
Jimmy says, "Try this . . ."
I say, "I don't need it!"
Jimmy says, "Try this . . .
Come on and try this!"
I say, "I don't think I need it!"

Sometimes it's just no fun
To feel like you're the only one
Who doesn't go along
When something seems wrong.
But they're not my friends if they can't see
I don't like people pushing me!

"Hey, what's the matter with you?"
"Come on, man! Everybody's going!"
"Chicken!"
"Nobody'll ever know."
"What are you, scared?"
"Everybody does it."

I might hang out with Jim,
But I don't need to be just like him.
Got to listen to myself,
'Cause you can't let someone else
Always make your move for you!
Got to find out what *you* want to do!

Doris Knows Everything

by Whoopi Goldberg
Illustrated by Gary Zamchick

Today I went to the Welfare Office with my mom. My friend Doris said that only really poor people who didn't take baths and ate out of garbage cans were at Welfare.

My friend Doris knows everything.

My friend Doris said that when you get there, there are these big doors and then you have to open them and they're really hard and you have to push until you sweat and then you have to walk down this big long hallway in the dark and they don't even give you a flashlight. And it's really cold in there and they don't even give you a sweater.

My friend Doris said you have to sit on a big tall stool and then they call your name and then you have to go into this room and there's a lady with big glasses and warts and fangs and that's what Doris said.

So I didn't want to go but my mother said I had to and I went. But you know, it looked just like any other building with real regular doors. I said, "Hmmmm."

We went in and there were some chairs and lots of people. I even knew some people. Those people that I knew didn't eat out of garbage cans. Mr. Kellis worked in the school I go to. He smiled and I said hello. I played with my friend Kasha; she was there too. Her mom plays with a symphony, but she got laid off.

And then they called our name and I got scared. And we went in to see a lady named Miss Mason. But she didn't have fangs or warts or glasses or anything. She was kinda pretty.

And I started to think about the things Doris said and I felt pretty silly for listening to her.

So when it was over, me and my mom went to the bathroom 'cause my mom always makes me go to the bathroom right before I leave anywhere because every time we go somewhere I say I have to go to the bathroom. And when we came out of the bathroom, guess who was sitting there with her mom—Doris.

I said, "Hi, Doris." Doris didn't say anything, she just hung her head.

I guess Doris doesn't know everything.

G. ZAMCHICK

Yourself Belongs to You

a rap song by The Fat Boys:
Damon Wimbley, Darren Robinson,
and Mark Morales, with Jimmy Glenn

Take AN-y PATH you WANT to,
  but one THING you OUGHT-a KNOW:
Don't let OTH-ers LEAD you PLACE-es
  YOU don't want to GO!
A DEF thing to re-MEM-ber
  if you DON'T know what to DO:
You GOT a RIGHT to STAND-ing TALL,
  Your-SELF be-LONGS to YOU!

Now . . .

We get ac-CUSED of ACT-in' STU-pid,
  and mak-IN' a LOT-ta NOISE,
But here's SOME-thing REAL SER-ious
  from the THREE FAT BOYS!
Now, one DAY you MIGHT get NERV-ous,
  OR FEEL PRES-sure
FROM SOME-ONE
  who might TRY to TAKE your MEAS-ure!
Some-BOD-y might PUSH you
  TO THE BRINK,
But DON'T BE a-FRAID!
  YO! STOP and THINK
a-BOUT this THING we've LEARNED
  (and WE'LL pass it a-LONG):
TRUST your-SELF! You KNOW the DEAL!
And you'll NEV-er GO WRONG!

You got BOD-y AND SPIR-it!
  WORD! They MAKE YOU u-NIQUE!
Any-ONE tries to de-STROY 'em,
  THEY ARE WEAK!

You got a RIGHT to FEEL GOOD—
  if you're BLUE OR SAD
From SOME-one HIT-tin' ON you—
  THEY'RE the ONE who's BAD!
YO! HURT-in' is con-FUS-in'
  'cause THERE'S so MAN-y WAYS
Other PEOP-le CAN FIND
  to MESS WITH your DAY;
But if they're ILL-in' WITH your HEART
  or BOD-y OR MIND;
If they PUT you in a BIND,
  it's O-ver THE LINE!
So keep UP your CON-fidence
  and DON'T FEEL LOW,
You've GOT a BRAIN like EIN-STEIN,
  JUST LET it SHOW!
You've got a HEART the SIZE of JUP-iter,
  so, CAN'T no-BOD-y HURT ya!
Your HEART's what TELLS you
  YOU ARE RIGHT;
  IT'll NEV-er JERK ya!

Take AN-y PATH you WANT to,
  but one THING you OUGHT-a KNOW:
Don't let OTH-ers LEAD your PLACE-es
  YOU don't want to GO!
A DEF thing to re-MEM-ber
  if you DON'T know what to DO:
You GOT a RIGHT to STAND-ing TALL,
  Your-SELF be-LONGS to YOU!

Just LET the FAT BOYS GIVE you
  a RULE OR TWO,
If some-BOD-y's TOUCH-in'-PULL-in'-
  PICK-in'-HIT-tin' ON YOU—
You don't WANT to be a-LONE?
  GO WITH your CREW!
And IF they STILL are FRONT-in',
  HERE'S WHAT you DO:
Just TELL 'em, "YO! STOP!"
  Then TELL 'em A-GAIN,
You're SICK AND TIRED
  of ALL their MESS-IN'!
And if THAT DON'T WORK,
  get some-ONE you TRUST,

Like your AUNT-ie or your TEACH-er,
  and let THEM MAKE the BUST!

Now we don't SAY when FRIENDS or FAM-i-ly
  MAKE YOU DO
SOME-thing YOU DON'T LIKE
  that they're MIS-TREAT-in' YOU!
They got a RIGHT to TURN you 'ROUND
  if you've GONE A-STRAY,
But if they're TOY-in' WITH your BOD-y,
  DON'T YOU PLAY!
They're like AN-y OTH-er STRANG-er,
  if you're BE-in' A-BUSED;
If the PILL's TOO BIG to SWAL-low,
  JUST RE-FUSE!
So, no MAT-ter WHO IT IS,
  don't TREAT THEM SOFT!
WORD UP, homeboy! GET MAD, flygirl!
  TELL 'em, "STEP OFF!"
'Cause WHEN the HEAT is IN your HOUSE,
  THAT'S the HOT-test YET,
So, go ELSE-where to GET re-LIEF;
But GET IT! BET!
What's RIGHT is RIGHT in BLACK and WHITE,
  NOTH-in' ELSE will DO.
You GOT a RIGHT to STAND-ing TALL,
  Your-SELF be-LONGS to YOU!

Lily Tomlin's Edith Ann in "And That's the Truth"

written and illustrated by Jane Wagner

"God has a TV set and
watches us on it.
Whenever I feel God
watching me,
I sing and dance and do
a commercial for myself."

"Sometimes when I feel nobody cares…
I go down to Sears and tell them
I'm lost and they call my name out
over the loudspeaker over and over.

We all need to feel like we matter.

I matter to Sears even though most of my clothes
come from J.C. Penney."

On My Pond

Words and Music Kermit the Frog
with Sarah Durkee and Christopher Cerf
Illustrations by Tom Cooke

♪ see page 168 for the music

There's a place where I can sit,
  just me, myself and I . . .
On my pond,
On my pond

Where the water's fresh and clean
  and peaceful as a sigh . . .
On my pond,
On my pond

Look at the grass all around me,
It's green as the smile on my face,
Look at the trees, they astound me!
Wow, what a byoo-tiful plaaace!

There's a spot where no one lives
    but quiet little fish . . .
On my pond,
On my pond.

Nature lets me come and visit
    any time I wish . . .
On my pond,
On my pond.

Look at us ALL, . . .
    we're enjoying
A breath of sweet country air . . .
Hey, this is getting ANNOYING!
PLEASE KEEP IT DOWN OVER THEEEERE . . . !

WAIT A MINUTE, WHO SAID YOU COULD
    DUMP YOUR GARBAGE HERE? . . .
On my pond,
On my pond.

CLEANIN' IT ALL UP AGAIN
    COULD TAKE US YEARS AND YEARS . . .
On my pond,
On my pond.

Keepin' it clean to BEGIN WITH!
Yes, that's the smart thing to do!
Don't let 'em cover our fins with
Any more black slimy gooooo . . . !

Save a place where I can sit,
   just me, myself and I. . . .
On my pond,
On my pond.

Keep the water fresh and clean
   and peaceful as a sigh . . .
On my pond,
On my pond!

All Us Come Cross the Water

by Lucille Clifton
Illustrated by John Steptoe

I got this teacher name Miss Wills. This day she come asking everybody to tell where they people come from. Everybody from over in the same place suppose to stand up by theirselves. When it come to me I don't say nothing so she get all mad, cause that make all the other brothers not say nothing too.

"Won't you please cooperate with us, Jim?" she say. I didn't say nothing cause my name is Ujamaa for one thing. So when the bell ring she ask me to stay a little after, so we can talk.

"We must not be ashamed of ourselves, Jim," she says. "You are from a great heritage and you must be proud of that heritage. Now you know you are from Africa, don't you?" she says.

I say, "Yes, mam," and walk on out the place.

First thing, my name is Ujamaa and also Africa is a continent not a country and she says she want everybody to tell what country. Anyhow, I left. The other brothers waiting for me by the light.

Malik say, "That woman is crazy. She get on my nerves."

Bo say, "How come we didn't stan up, Ujamaa? We from Africa!" I just go on home. Bo don't know nothing.

I got a sister name Rose. She studying to be a practical nurse. When she get home I ask her, "Rose where we from?" She come talking about, "Mama was from Rome, Georgia, and Daddy from Birmingham."

"Before that," I say.

"Mama's Daddy from Georgia too."

"I mean before that too, way back before that." She come laughing talking about, "They wasn't no way back before that. Before that we was a slave."

Rose make me sick.

My Daddy's name Nat. He work for the city. When he get home I ask him, "Daddy where we from?"

He say, "What you talking about, boy?"

I say, "I wanna know where did we come from."

133

He say, "We come up here from Birmingham after your Mama died."
"I mean back before that."
"Boy, I'm too tired to fool with you. Go ask Big Mama these questions."
Big Mama is my Mama's Mama's Mama. She real old and she don't say much, but she see things cause she born with a veil over her face. That make it so she can see spirits and things.
I go up to her and I ask her, "Big Mama, where we come from?"
She say, "Why you wanna know?"
I tell her about the teacher and everybody.
She say, "My Mama say her and her Mama was brought from Whydah in Dahomey in 1855." She say, "My Mama was nine years old."
"That mean I'm from Whydah?"
She look at me then.
"Your Daddy's people look like Ashanti people. They come from south in Ghana."
"That mean I'm from Ashanti people?"
She say, "Who are you, boy?"

I say, "I'm Ujamaa."

Shoot, she know who I am, it was her give me my name.

She say, "Go on now then. I'm through."

That's how she is.

I got a grown man friend over to the Panther Book Shop. Everybody call him Tweezer. We talk about things sometime and I tell him what I'm gonna be and all that. He always say, "Just you be a good brother, Ujamaa." Anyhow, I thought I'd go on over and talk to him about things and everything. I waited till after dinner cause we had red beans which I love. Rose don't like old Tweezer much so when she ask me where am I going I tell her over to Bo's. She remind me to be home when the lights go on.

Tweezer sitting out in front of the store, got his wine in a paper cup. He old but not as old as Big Mama. People talk about he used to run on the road and before that he went to college. He real smart. He know it too always talkin about he a juju man, know all about magic and stuff like that. He see me coming down the block and wave.

"Hey, Ujamaa," he kinda grinned.

"Hey, Tweezer," I grinned back.

When I got up to the store he made room for me on the bench. He didn't say nothing. He never do start first.

I say, "What's your real name, Tweezer?"

He say, "I don't know."

"How come?"

"It got left."

I say, "Where?"

He say, "In Africa."

"What you mean?"

"When they stole my Daddy's Daddy to make him a slave they didn't ask for his name and he didn't give it."

"Well what did they call him?"

He say, "Whatever he let um. Reckon he figure if they ain't got his name they ain't really got him."

I say, "Big Mama give me my name. It mean Unity." He smile then. He start really talking.

"Long as your own give you the name you know it's yours. We name us. Everybody else just calling us something, but we name us. You named a good name."

I ask him, "Tweezer, we from all different parts of Africa, how we gonna say what country we from?"

Tweezer say, "We from all them countries, Ujamaa. All off the same boat."

I say, "Some people tell me we wasn't all slaves."

He say, "Wasn't none of us free though. All us crossed the water. We one people, Ujamaa. Boy got that name oughta know that. All us crossed the water."

The lights had to come on just then.

I told Tweezer, "See you later."

"Just be a good brother, brother," Tweezer told me.

Man, I had a whole lot to think about! I'm suppose to lay real still cause I sleep with my Daddy and he got to go to work but Man my mind was going to town. Thing was, what I mostly ended up thinking about was ol Bo and ol Malik and how they didn't even know what was the matter but they went right along with me on the not standing up cause we brothers. And Bo ain't

even lived in this block that long and his Mama is from the islands but we all brothers anyhow. I thought about Tweezer and him and me being brothers too. All us come cross the water. Somebody name Ujamaa oughta know that. I went on to sleep.

Next day everybody in class looking at me seeing what am I gonna do. Miss Wills got her mouth all sad think I'm shamed of something. Pretty soon she say,

"Let us continue yesterday's social studies lesson, children. We will excuse Jim from the lesson this time."

Just when she say that I jump up and stand straight as a king, and look right at her and say,

"Miss Wills, my name is Ujamaa and that mean Unity and that's where I'm from." Man, Malik and Bo stand right up too, tall as me and just grinning. We all stand there awhile and she don't say nothing. Shoot, she don't even know what we talking about!

Something for Everyone

Words and Music by Carol Hall
Illustrated by Seymour Chwast

♪ see page 169 for the music

Something for everyone,
that's when a family's fun.
There's lots of surprises,
with different sizes
and shapes to a family.
Something for sharing there,
with people caring there.
It's a door you can go in,
a place you can grow in.
It's anything you need it to be.

Maybe it's your mother and your dad and you.
Maybe you have one place or divide it in two.
Maybe there's a brother or a sis who shares.
Maybe there's a grandma with a room upstairs.
Maybe there's an aunt with all her children grown.
Maybe there's a stepdad with kids of his own.
Maybe there's a cousin, even three or four,
sleeping all together on one great big floor.
But there's

Something for everyone,
that's when a family's fun.
There's lots of surprises,
with different sizes
and shapes to a family.
Something for sharing there,
with people caring there.
It's a door you can go in,
a place you can grow in.
It's anything you need it to be.

Living in a castle or a riverboat,
living in a farmhouse with a billy goat,
living in an igloo or an Indian tent,
living in a small apartment—paying rent,
living on a mountain where the sky is blue,
living in a one-room with a window view. . . .
No, it's not the people or the place they live.
It's more the kind of feeling and the love they give.
But there's

Something for everyone,
that's when a family's fun.
There's lots of surprises,
with different sizes
and shapes to a family.
Something for sharing there,
with people caring there.
It's a door you can go in,
a place you can grow in.
It's anything you need it to be.

Something for everyone!

The Kingdom with No Rules, No Laws, and No King

by Norman Stiles
Illustrated by Arnie Levin

Once upon a time a young boy named Benjamin lived in a kingdom that had no rules and no laws of any kind.

It also had no king . . . but let's not get into that now.

It did have: majestic mountain ranges, roaring rivers, really cool castles, cutesy cottages, beautiful birds and adorable furry animals, great weather, miles of beaches, perfect waves, all kinds of excellent trees great for climbing, and a more than adequate number of benches for people to sit on.

One day, Benjamin was sitting on one of these benches with his father, mother, and big sister. He was wearing a cowboy hat, and they were all eating chocolate ice cream cones. All of a sudden, a guy walked up to Benjamin, did a sort of silly dance, took Benjamin's cone right out from under his tongue, and ran off licking it.

"Hey! That guy took my chocolate ice cream cone!" Ben yelled.

"I noticed," said his father, licking his own ice cream. "He made a nice move on you."

"Guess he was in the mood for some chocolate ice cream, dear," said his mother sweetly.

"You have to learn not to pay attention to silly dances when you're eating ice cream," his big sister said.

Remember, this was a kingdom without rules or laws of *any* kind. So, there were no rules or laws about taking ice cream cones that didn't belong to you.

Benjamin still wanted more ice cream. So he reached over and took his sister's cone.

She immediately and matter-of-factly snatched her mother's cone.

Benjamin's father quickly gulped *his* ice cream down in one bite just as Ben's mother was about to grab it.

"Ha, ha!" he said, with a big chocolate moustache dripping from his upper lip.

Benjamin's mother sat thinking for a moment as Ben and his sister licked their ice cream very fast, keeping one eye on their mother.

Then, Benjamin's mother started to whistle and appeared to be about to scratch an itch on her head. Instead, she reached around her daughter, knocked Benjamin's ice cream cone out of his hand up in the air, and caught it in her mouth.

Benjamin sighed a very deep sigh and said to himself, "There's got to be a better way."

His sister and his mother finished their ice cream cones. Then everyone put on their crash helmets, got in the car, and with Benjamin's mother at the wheel, the family headed home. Ben wore his cowboy hat on top of his helmet.

There were no traffic laws of any kind. So as their car approached the kingdom's main intersection, Benjamin's mother had a decision to make. If the light was red, she could stop if she felt like it or she didn't have to if she didn't feel like it. If it was green, she could stop or she could go if she felt like it.

The light was green, and Benjamin's mother decided that she felt like going through it. Unfortunately, the person in the truck in front of her felt like *stopping* for the green light.

Just before the car smashed into the rear of the truck, Benjamin thought to himself, "There's *got* to be a better way!"

The next thing he knew, he was hanging by one leg, upside down, from a branch near the top of a very, very tall tree. And this was *not* one of the trees in the kingdom that was great for climbing.

"They're gonna need ladders and stuff to get me down," he thought to himself. He was going to be up there for a while so he decided that the best thing to do was to relax.

He looked around and saw that his parents and his big sister were each hanging by one leg, upside down, in trees, as were lots of other people all around the intersection.

Everyone looked relaxed and nobody was particularly peeved. That was because they were used to it. Most of the many automobile accidents in the kingdom with no rules and no laws resulted in people hanging by one leg, upside down, in trees.

As Benjamin swayed in the breeze, he could see a baseball field in the distance. A game was in progress, a game with no rules, of course. The players were doing whatever they felt like doing. Some were swinging bats. Some were throwing balls. Some were catching balls.

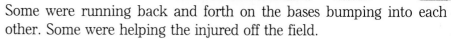

Some were running back and forth on the bases bumping into each other. Some were helping the injured off the field.

There was no score for some, and for others it was 12 to 6 or 765 to 125 and so on.

For some a hit was a hit, for others a hit was an out, and for a few there was no such thing as a hit or an out.

Some just sort of sat there in the middle of the base paths, digging in the dirt with pails and shovels.

"THERE'S GOT TO BE A BETTER WAY!" Benjamin was screaming over and over as they carried him down from the tree.

"It's okay, Benjamin, dear. You're down now," his mother said. "We're all okay now. We're out of our trees. See. We're out of our trees!"

Benjamin looked around and saw that everyone was, indeed, out of their trees. And it was at that very moment that he resolved to himself he would figure out a better way.

"I'm going to my room and I'm not coming out until I'm finished!" Benjamin said.

"Finished with what?" his sister asked.

"I don't know yet," he said, slamming the door behind him.

News spread all over the kingdom that a boy named Benjamin had gone to his room and wouldn't come out until he was finished. The entire kingdom gathered around Benjamin's house waiting for him to come out of his room with whatever it was that he was finishing.

Then, after two and a half hours, Benjamin emerged.

"Finished!" he said.

"Finished *what*?" the kingdom asked.

"Three laws and a bunch of rules," he said proudly.

"Huh?" said the kingdom, not having the faintest idea what he was talking about.

"This is the bunch of rules," Benjamin explained, holding up a booklet. "From now on, we'll play baseball by the rules in this book, like nine people on each side, nine innings, four balls, three strikes, no pails and shovels, stuff like that. If you don't play by these rules, you can't play."

"Interesting!" some of the people in the kingdom said.

"Sounds pretty good," others said.

"No pails and shovels? Phooey!" said Benjamin's mother and father and some others.

"Get to the three laws!" his sister demanded impatiently.

"Yeah!" said the kingdom.

"Okay," Benjamin said, and he took out a very impressive piece of notebook paper and began to read:

"Everyone will stop on red and go on green. That's the first law.

"Nobody can take another person's chocolate ice cream cone. That's the second law.

"Every day at noon, the entire kingdom has to come over to my house, play cowboy, dig in my sandbox with pails and shovels, and sing and dance to a great song I wrote called 'Hail Benjamin, He's a Heck of a Guy!' That's the third law. If you don't obey the laws, you get punished."

"Interesting," some of the people in the kingdom said.

"Sounds pretty good!" others said.

"The law with the pails and shovels is my favorite," said Benjamin's mother and father.

"Hail *who*?" said a guy in the back to no one in particular.

Then Benjamin said that he was going back to his room and he would not come out until the kingdom tried the three laws and the bunch of rules.

So they did. And they found that they no longer spent as much time hanging by one leg, upside down, in trees. They were able to finish their chocolate ice cream cones, and baseball was a lot more fun. But every day at noon, not everyone was coming over to Benjamin's house and playing cowboy, digging, and singing and dancing like they were supposed to.

"I can't. I have an earache," one guy said.

"I'm allergic," said another guy.

"My pail and shovel are at the cleaners," Ben's sister said.

"Oh yeah?" said Benjamin. "Prove it. Show me doctors' notes and a pail-and-shovel cleaning ticket."

The two guys had notes, but Benjamin's sister didn't have a pail-and-shovel cleaning ticket. She said she'd lost it. Then she said, "Okay, look. I don't like the third law. I don't see why, every day at noon, everyone has to come all the way over to our house and play cowboy, dig, and sing and dance to 'Hail Benjamin, He's a Heck of a Guy!' "

"We have to because it's the law," the kingdom tried to explain.

"But it's a *silly* law. It serves no useful purpose," Benjamin's sister replied.

"True," Benjamin said. "But I like it a lot. It's a *fun* law!"

His parents agreed.

"I don't think it's fun!" Benjamin's sister said. "I don't like it one bit."

"You don't?" Benjamin asked.

"No, I don't!" said his sister.

To Benjamin's genuine surprise, more than a few of the people in the kingdom appeared to agree with her.

"Okay, no problem," Benjamin said with a shrug. "From now on, the law is: Every day at noon, *no one's* allowed to come over to our house and do *anything*."

"Brilliant! Hooray for Benjamin!" cheered everyone in the kingdom. Everyone except Benjamin's sister, that is.

"Wait a minute! That's no good either!" she shouted, taking a deep breath. "We don't need a law to force people to come over to our house and play cowboy and dig and sing and stuff like that, but we also shouldn't have one to *stop* them from doing it if they feel like it."

"We shouldn't?" the kingdom asked.

"No," she said. "As long as no harm comes to anyone, why should there be a law against it?"

"You know, she has a point," said her mother and father.

"A very *good* point!" a lot of other people in the kingdom joined in.

So the kingdom kept the first and second laws and the bunch of rules, but got rid of the third law altogether. They also decided that from then on, *all* the people would be involved in making laws and rules because, after all, stuff like that was just too important to be left to some guy in a cowboy hat.

Benjamin eventually became a very successful singing cowboy. His sister became senior partner of the kingdom's first law firm. His parents became umpires. And the kingdom that now had *some* laws and *some* rules lived lawfully ever after. It still had no king . . . but it's too late to get into that now.

THE END

The Turn of the Tide

*Words and Music by Carly Simon
and Jacob Brackman
Illustrated by John Steptoe*

♪ see page 170 for the music

How can we know
   the fate of the earth?
Must everything go
   from bad to worse?
How can we be
   just along for the ride?
We'd rather believe
   that WE decide!
That we can stand here
And say loud and clear:
   Here comes the turn of the tide.

Here comes the turn,
Here comes the turn,
Here comes the turn of the tide.

We cannot go on
   sounding alarms
And rattling swords
   and building bombs
And fouling the air
   and the streams underground.
We've got to begin
   to turn it around!
It's our right to be heard,
Our right to decide—
Here comes the turn of the tide.

Here comes the turn,
Here comes the turn,
Here comes the turn of the tide.

We Need a Bigger Turkey

by Christopher Cerf and Norman Stiles
Illustrated by Chris Demarest

One day my dad took Mom and Sid
And Sue and me aside,
And he said, "Let's have a party!
Hey! Let's show our family pride!
We've got such a loving family!
We've got lots to celebrate!
So let's eat the biggest turkey
That five people ever ate!"

Then Dad telephoned our butcher
(Who's a woman named Marie),
And he told her 'bout the turkey
And how big it had to be.

"Sounds great!" said Mom, when Dad hung up,
"But I don't think it's fair
To have a family feast
If Gramps and Grandma aren't there."
"Good point!" said Sue, "and how 'bout
Aunt Elaine and Uncle Gus?
Last time *they* served a turkey
They invited all of *us.*"

"You're right, of course," my father said,
"And when you add each cousin,
The number in our party
Will have reached an even dozen."

So Dad called back the butcher,
And he passed along the word;
"Gonna need a bigger turkey!
Gonna need a larger bird!
'Cause the guest list for our dinner
Has had seven added to it.
Please, Marie, ya gotta help us!"
And the butcher said, "I'll do it!"

Just then, my little brother Sid
Began to scream and pout.
He said, "Dad, I love our babysitter!
Please don't leave her out!"
"And we've *got* to ask the neighbors,"
Mother added lovingly.
"Sure, I know we're not *related,*
But they're family to me!"

So Dad called up the butcher,
And he said, "Remember me?
Well, we need a bigger turkey,
We'll be feeding fifty-three!"

And the butcher said, "No problem!
Hey, don't sweat it, have no fear!
You need a bird for fifty-three?
I've got that bird right here!"

Then Sue brought up the club she runs
That works for conservation,
And Dad his bowling league,
And Mom her Children's Aid Foundation.
And we thought of tons of other folks
We all hold close and dear.
Said Dad, "No doubt about it,
All those people should be here!"

So he called the butcher up and sighed,
"I hate to be a bother,
But it seems our party's grown again.
I'm sorry!" said my father.

"We're gonna host a thousand people,
Give or take a few.
We need a bigger turkey,
And it all depends on you!"

And the butcher said, "I've *just* the bird
To feed the guests you've got.
Your turkey got here yesterday.
It's in the parking lot!"

Well, everyone seemed pleased,
But then I said, "For what it's worth,
The *world* is one big family
'Cause we all share *just one earth*."

"Good point!" said Mom and Dad,
"Our party won't be a success
Unless we invite *everyone,*
And everyone says yes."

So Dad called back the butcher,
And she said, "Now let me guess.
You need a bigger turkey?"
And my father answered, "Yes.

"A bird to feed five billion mouths
Or more before we're through."
"No bird's that big," the butcher sighed,
"I'm sorry. No can do!"

We all burst into tears
When we heard about the call,
And how the largest turkey
In the world was still too small.

But suddenly my mom cried, "Wait!
We won't throw in the towel!
If we can't *buy* the bird we need,
We'll make our *own* big fowl!"

Well, it's taken years of carving,
And of ordering from delis,
But at last we've got a gobbler
That'll fill five billion bellies.
So, world, you're all invited,
Come by air, land, sea, or river,
And taste the biggest turkey
Ever sculpted from chopped liver!

We and They

by Lucille Clifton
Illustrated by Jerry Pinkney

Boris and Yuki and Sarah and Sue
and Karl and Latanya, Maria too
dreamed of the world
and it was spinning
and all the people
just talked about winning.
The wind was burning.
The water was churning.
The trees were bending.
Something was ending
and all the talk was "we" and "they."
The children all hugged themselves
waiting for the day
when the night of the long bad dream
is done
and all the family of humans
are one
and being and winning are not the same
and "we" and "they" is just a game
and the wind is a friend that
doesn't fuss
and every They is
actually Us.

Thank Someone

Words by Sarah Durkee, Music by Paul Jacobs
Illustrated by James McMullan

♪ see page 171 for the music

Mom put down the paper
just to help me find my shoe.
Kim likes chocolate doughnuts,
so her cousin gave her two.
Grampa played with Julio,
took him to the park.
If you forgot to thank someone,
say thank you in the dark.

Thank the moon,
thank the sun,
most of all
Thank someone.
Thank the stars
high above,
one for
everyone you love.

Gretchen taught a funny song
to Jack and Eleanor.
Ed brought Andy comics
when he had to stay indoors.
Mrs. Rose helped Dana
when she waded out too deep.
If you forgot to thank someone,
say thank you in your sleep.

Thank the moon,
thank the sun,
most of all
Thank someone.
Thank the stars
high above,
one for
everyone you love.

Friends are like a family,
and families are like friends.
All the world's your family;
the chain will never end.
When the night is lonely
and we're feelin' miles apart,
if you forgot to thank someone
say thank you in your heart.

Thank the moon,
thank the sun,
most of all
Thank someone.
Thank the stars
high above,
one for
everyone you love.

Friendly Neighborhood, Words and Music by Lynn Ahrens and Stephen Flaherty

gran - ny, 'cause now there's Grand-ma Pam.___ And I'm not Mom and

Dad are do - ing fine, And Sam and me are do - ing fine, and, hey, we feel a whole lot bet - ter than I

ev - er thought we would! I mean, o - kay, my fam - i - ly split, but now, the piec-es kind-a fit...and it's like

liv - ing in the mid - dle of a friend-ly neigh - bor - hood!

(spoken:) And you know what? Best thing of all? They all like me!

Jimmy Says, Words and Music by David Buskin and Abra Bigham

♩ = 105 Driving Dance Beat

CHORUS

1. Jim-my says,"Do this..." Jim-my says, "Do this..." I say, "I don't want to!"
2. Jim-my says,"Try this..." Jim-my says, "Try this..." I say, "I don't need it!"
3. (spoken:) (Girl:) "Hey, what's the matter with you?" (Boy:) "Come on, man! Everybody's

"Jim-my says,"Do this..." "Jim-my says, "Do this..." I say, "I don't want to!"
"Jim-my says,"Try this... Come on and try this!" I say, "I don't think I need it!"
going!" (Boy) "Chicken!" (Girl:) "Nobody'll ever know." (Girl:) "What are you, scared?" (Boy:) "Everybody

VERSE

Trying to make up my own mind,___ Got my own di - rec - tion to find!
Some-times it's just no fun___ To feel like you're the on - ly one___
does it!" (sung) I might hang out with Jim,___ But I don't need to be___ just like him...

Yeah, I know Jim-my's cool, And ev'ry-one in school___ u-
Who does-n't go a - long When some-thing seems wrong.___ But they're
Got to lis - ten to my-self, 'Cause you can't let some-one else

su-al-ly does what Jim-my does___ With-out think-ing, just be-cause ___
not my friends if they can't see___ I don't like peo - ple push-ing me!___
Al - ways make your move for you! Got to find out what you want to do!

3rd time - D.C. & fade

158

It's Not My Fault, Words and Music by Sarah Durkee and Christopher Cerf

♩ = 135 Animated Rock

VERSE

1. Mom and Dad are mad to-night, The din-ner ta-ble's si-lent, My
2. May-be I should tell a joke, Make ev-'ry-bod-y laugh, But

sis-ter's get-tin' crab-by and my broth-er's get-tin' vio-lent! Things __ are look-in' bad to-night, It's
ev-'ry time I tell one, I for-get the sec-ond half! __ May __ be they're all sick of me For

real-ly plain to see, And I don't know just who's to blame, But don't go blam-in' me! 'Cause It's
be-in' such a jerk, Or may-be Dad's just tir-ed, May-be Mom's just o-ver-worked. Well, It's

CHORUS

Not My Fault! No, It's Not __ My Fault!
    1. My
    2. That
    3. I

fam-i-ly bit my head off, And all I said was "Pass the salt!" __
no one's say-in' noth-in' 'Cause they don't have noth-in' nice to say! __
know I'm not the one Who put my fam-i-ly in a rot-ten mood! __

Hey, It's }
Hey, It's } Not My Fault! No, It's Not My Fault!
Yeah, It's }

When no one else is talk-in', I just tell my-self It's Not My Fault! __
When no one else is talk-in', I just tell my-self that I'm o-kay! __
And just be-cause we're fight-ing Does-n't mean we're gon-na come un-glued!

1. __
2. __
You

BRIDGE

might be be-ing per-fect, Might be act-in' good as gold, But some-times peo-ple fight no mat-ter

what you try to do! We catch each oth-er's an-ger Like we catch each oth-er's cold. That's

when you got to tell your-self it's not be-cause of you! It's

D.S. to 3rd Chorus
repeat & fade

In My Room, Words and Music by Bobby Gosh

I'm Never Afraid, Words and Music by Sarah Durkee and Christopher Cerf

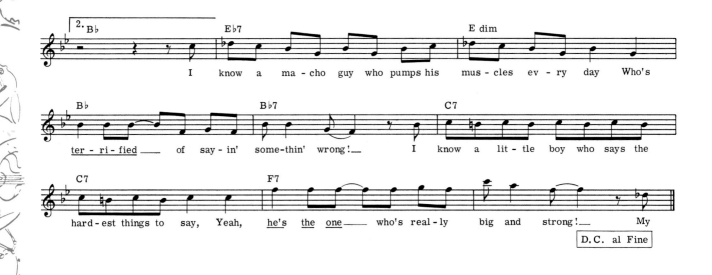

I know a ma-cho guy who pumps his mus-cles ev-ry day Who's

ter - ri-fied ___ of say-in' some-thin' wrong! ___ I know a lit-tle boy who says the

hard-est things to say, Yeah, he's the one ___ who's real-ly big and strong! ___ My

D.C. al Fine

The Stupid Song, Words and Music by Robin Batteau

♩=161 New Orleans "Zydeco" Style

A CHORUS

1. Brother:
2. Sister:
3. Mom & Dad:
4. The Family:

Ev - 'ry-thing's so stu - pid, stu-pid, stu-pid, stu-pid, stu - pid, stu-pid, stu-pid, And I

(3.) we

hate it, hate it, hate it, hate it, hate it, hate it, May-be if I say it, say it, say it, say it,

(3.) we

say it to my - self, I won't have to yell ___ at my

1. mom.
2. dad.
3. our kids.
4. ... THEM!

(3.) our - selves, We

fine

VERSE

1. Be - in' a kid ___ is no bowl of cher - ries, No bed of ros - es, No
2. Be - in' a kid ___ is no laugh-ing mat - ter, No sil - ver plat - ter, No
3. Be - in' a grown - up's no spring pic - nic, No day at the beach, No

piece of cake. ___ When I act like a grown - up, They say I'm pre-co - cious. When I
yel-low brick road. ___ When I say what I think, They say "Kid ___ you're too young."
eas - y street. ___ E - ven if you're mak-in' their fav - 'rite treat, ___ You can

1. 2. 3.

act like a kid, ___ They tell me that I'm hope - less.
And when I'm quiet, They say, "Cat got your tongue?" ___
lead your kids to lunch But you can't make 'em eat! ___

Ev - 'ry-thing's so

D.S. al fine

some-thing's wrong. Come on, what is it? You'd be sur-prised— How pres-sures rise The more—

(sung:)

— you hide Be-hind— your pride— Don't keep things bot-tled up in-side._____ We'll

CHORUS

both feel bet-ter if we talk it o - ver. We'll both feel bet-ter if we talk. We'll

both feel bet-ter if we talk it o - ver. We'll both feel bet-ter if we talk. Talk it o -

- ver,____ talk it o - ver,____ talk it o - ver, ___ talk it o - ver.____

Mom: (M:) ("RAP" VERSE 4 - figure plays 7 times)

Quit it! I ad-mit it! I real-ly got up tight! It start-ed out friend-ly, but it turned in-to a fight. When he

took me to a rest-aurant, I knew it was-n't right. At first I was read-y to bask in his praise,

Read-y to thank him and ask for a raise. But he said, "Costs are up, sales are in a rut." So would I

Daughter: (D:)   (M:)

vol - un - teer____ to kind-ly take a cut??? But you've worked so hard.... What a pay off! He

(D:)

threat-ened me with a pos-i-ble lay-off! The man's a dweeb,_ and that's a fact! * You're

(M:)   (D:)   (M:)

al - ways so con-cerned with how a mom's sup-posed to act. Yeah... Were you scared that I'd be scared? Yeah,

(M: & D:)

e - ven though you know I know__ We need to share what needs to be shared!_ (sung:) We'll

* Mom (crying in background): "I swore I wouldn't worry you..."

D.S. repeat Chorus & fade

From Here to Forever, Words and Music by Kris Kristofferson, Stephen Bruton, Glen Clark, and Billy Swan

The Biggest Problem (Is in Other People's Minds), Words and Music by Don Haynie

♩ = 87 Uptempo Country

1. My broth-er Bob-by nev-er list-ens when I talk; Pays close at-ten-tion though, and
2. I've known Ros-a for a year or so by now; We've been all a-round, I
3. An-gie reads to me the po-et-ry she loves; Hands brush the pag-es with the

watch-es like a hawk. Took some time for my hands to learn the signs, But now the
some-times won-der how. The doors and the stairs give us trou-ble with her chair; It may take
gen-tle-ness of doves. Sings me a song from the pia-no clear and strong, She's nev-er

two of us, we get a-long just fine. Bob-by's big-gest prob-lem is in
long-er, but we go ev-'ry-where. Ros-a's big-gest prob-lem is in
seen me, yet she's known me all a-long. An-gie's big-gest prob-lem is in

oth-er peo-ple's minds; We do things we like to do and have a great time.
oth-er peo-ple's minds; We go where we want to go and have a great time.
oth-er peo-ple's minds; We go hik-ing, we go swim-ming, in the sum-mer sun-shine.

Some kids stay a-way, but if they knew him they would find Bob-by's big-gest prob-lem real-ly is in
Since this cit-y's build-ers did-n't think when they de-signed, Ros-a's big-gest prob-lem real-ly is in
An-y-one can see I'm luck-y she's a friend of mine, And that An-gie's big-gest prob-lem is in

1. 2.
oth-er peo-ple's minds.
oth-er peo-ple's minds.
3.
oth-er peo-ple's minds. Some-

times the big-gest prob-lem is in oth-er peo-ple's minds; Be ex-act-ly who you are, and

you'll do just fine. Things may look im-pos-si-ble, but try and you will find That the

big-gest prob-lem real-ly is in oth-er peo-ple's, oth-er peo-ple's—

Some-day we will change those peo-ple's minds!

On My Pond, Words and Music by Kermit the Frog, with Sarah Durkee and Christopher Cerf

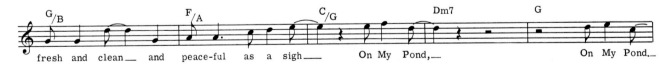

Something for Everyone, *Words and Music by Carol Hall*

Thank Someone, *Music by Paul Jacobs, Words by Sarah Durkee*

Afterword

by Kurt Vonnegut, Jr.

Until recent times human beings usually had a permanent community of relatives. They had dozens of homes to go to. So when a married couple had a fight, one or the other could go to a house three doors down and stay with a close relative until he or she was feeling tender again. Or if kids got so fed up with their parents that they couldn't stand it, they could march over to their uncle's for a while. Now this is rarely possible. Each family is locked into its little box. The neighbors aren't relatives. There aren't other houses where people can go and be cared for. When we ponder what's happening to America—"Where have the old values gone?" and all that—the answer is perfectly simple. We're lonesome. We don't have enough friends or relatives anymore. And we would if we lived in real communities.

It's a sunny little dream I have of a happier future. I couldn't survive my own pessimism if I didn't have some kind of sunny little dream. That's mine, and don't tell me I'm wrong: Human beings *will* be happier—when they find ways to be more comfortable together, to have more attitudes and experiences in common, to be more like genuine relatives. That's my utopia. That's what I want for you, me, and all of us.

About the Contributors

LYNN AHRENS (coauthor of "Friendly Neighborhood") has written music, lyrics and scripts for television, film and the stage. She has created and produced five Emmy-nominated children's television shows and, with collaborator Stephen Flaherty, won the 1987 Richard Rodgers Award for their musical, *Lucky Stiff*. Her children's TV songwriting credits include *Schoolhouse Rock* and *Captain Kangaroo*.

ROBIN BATTEAU (composer-lyricist of "The Stupid Song") is a songwriter whose work has been recorded by such artists as Anne Murray, Bette Midler, Tom Rush and Southside Johnny and the Asbury Jukes. He and fellow *Free To Be . . . A Family* contributor David Buskin sing and perform together as the folk/rock duo, Buskin and Batteau. One of six children of a rocket-scientist father and a concert-pianist mother, he was raised in Cambridge, Massachusetts. Mr. Batteau won the 1987 Clio Award for the best advertising song of the year, "The Heartbeat of America," which he wrote, arranged, performed, and produced for Chevrolet.

ABRA BIGHAM (coauthor of "Jimmy Says") is an actress, playwright and lyricist. She is the coauthor of *Mary S*, a musical drama based on the life of Mary Shelley, which won Grand Prize in the New Works Competition sponsored by the 1987 American Musical Theatre Festival. She has also received a George London Award from the National Institute for Music Theatre and two National Penwomen's Association prizes. Ms. Bigham grew up in Batesville, Indiana, with one brother, two sisters, and nineteen cousins of approximately similar age—an experience to which she attributes her expertise on peer pressure.

JACOB BRACKMAN (coauthor of "Talk It Over" and "The Turn of the Tide") is a former journalist (staff writer at *The New Yorker*, film critic of *Esquire* magazine) who has for some time worked in movies, theater and pop music. He has collaborated with Carly Simon for nearly twenty years. The hit songs they have written together include "That's the Way I Always Heard It Should Be." "Attitude Dancing" and "I Haven't Got Time for the Pain," which recently found new life as the theme song for a pain reliever.

STEPHEN BRUTON (coauthor of "From Here to Forever") has been the lead guitarist of Kris Kristofferson's long-standing back-up band, The Borderlords, since the early 1970s. A native of Fort Worth, Texas, he is a recent newlywed and now splits his nontouring time between homes in Austin, Texas and Malibu, California.

DAVID BUSKIN (coauthor of "Jimmy Says") is a Clio-Award-winning jingle writer and keyboard player who also records and performs as half of the folk/pop duo, Buskin and Batteau. He and partner Robin Batteau have made three successful albums, and have appeared in New York's Carnegie Hall, Boston's Symphony Hall and the Kennedy Center in Washington. Songs written or cowritten by Mr. Buskin have been recorded by Peter, Paul, and Mary, the Oak Ridge Boys, Bette Midler and Johnny Mathis. Mr. Buskin also writes humorous prose—three of his pieces were published in *Snooze*, a 1986 parody of *The New Yorker*.

ANN CAMERON ("The Night We Started Dancing") was born in Rice Lake, Wisconsin, and now lives in Panajachel, Guatemala. She is a children's author who has also taught, most recently as a creative writing professor at Queens College in New York. Her work, *The Stories Julian Tells*, was an American Library Association Notable Book and won a Parent's Choice Award. She is also a recipient of the Irma Simonton Black Award for children's literature. "The Night We Started Dancing" was inspired by a Christmas eve she spent with Guatemalan friends.

CHRISTOPHER CERF (editor of *Free To Be . . . A Family*; coauthor of "I'm Never Afraid," "It's Not My Fault," "On My Pond" and "We Need a Bigger Turkey") was the founding editor-in-chief of *Sesame Street* Books, Records and Toys. Since 1970, he has written many songs for *Sesame Street* and its sister productions, *The Electric Company* and *Square One TV*, earning two Grammy Awards in the process. His book credits include *Kids: Day In and Day Out*, coedited with Elisabeth Scharlatt, which was nominated for an American Book Award in 1979, and *The Experts Speak*, which he wrote with Victor Navasky. He is a former contributing editor of *National Lampoon*, and he conceived and coedited the best-selling newspaper parody *Not The New York Times*.

EVE CHWAST (illustrator of "The Night We Started Dancing') is an artist whose specialties are three-dimensional papier-mâché sculptures and woodcuts. Before creating the woodcuts in this book, she studied dozens of photographs of the people and landscape of Guatemala taken by author Ann Cameron. Eve Chwast is the daughter of Seymour Chwast.

SEYMOUR CHWAST (designer-illustrator of the *Free To Be . . . A Family* book jacket and illustrator of "Something For Everyone") is a founding partner of Push Pin Studios, whose distinctive style has had a worldwide influence on contemporary visual communications. His designs and illustrations have been used in books, magazines, animated films, advertising, record covers, posters and packaging. Mr. Chwast and Push Pin were honored at a two-month retrospective exhibition at the Louvre entitled "The Push Pin Style," and his work is in the permanent collections of New York's Museum of Modern Art, the Cooper-Hewitt Museum of the Smithsonian Institution and the Library of Congress. He was the 1985 American Institute of Graphic Arts Gold Medalist and is a member of the Art Director's Hall of Fame. Seymour Chwast is the father of Eve Chwast.

GLEN CLARK (coauthor of "From Here To Forever") plays guitar, keyboards, and harmonica, and also supplies back-up vocals, for the Borderlords, Kris Kristofferson's back-up band. He and his wife, Joyce, live with their two children in Fort Worth, Texas.

LUCILLE CLIFTON (author of "We And They" and "All Us Come Cross the Water") is an award-winning poet and children's writer. Among her best-known works are the highly acclaimed Everett Anderson books, published by Holt, Rinehart and Winston. The mother of six children (and the grandmother of six more). Ms. Clifton is a professor of literature and creative writing at the University of California at Santa Cruz and is the former Poet Laureate of Maryland. Her poem "Three Wishes" appeared in *Free To Be . . . You and Me*.

TOM COOKE (illustrator of "Boy Meets Girl Plus One" and "On My Pond") has illustrated successful books for many publishers, including Random House, Golden Books and Parker Brothers. He first met Kermit the Frog and friends when he illustrated a *Sesame Street* game in the early 1970s and he has been a mainstay of *Sesame Street* and *Muppets* publications ever since. Mr. Cooke has won Merit Awards from the Society of Illustrators, The Design Institute of America and the Boston Art Director's Club. He and his wife, Onalee, spend part of each year in Manchester, Massachusetts, and the rest of it in Bermuda. They have two married sons.

CHRIS DEMAREST (illustrator of "The Entertainer" and "We Need a Bigger Turkey") is a cartoonist and artist whose work appears regularly in such national magazines as *Forbes*, *Redbook*, and *The Atlantic*. A resident of Stratham, New Hampshire, Mr. Demarest has also written and illustrated several of his own children's books, including *Orville's Odyssey* and *No Peas for Nellie*.

LEO AND DIANE DILLON (illustrators of "Cross Your Fingers") are a husband-and-wife team who have produced some of the most beautiful and evocative children's books available anywhere. They achieved the unprecedented honor of winning the Caldecott Medal in two consecutive years, for *Why Mosquitoes Buzz in People's Ears* (1976) and *Ashanti to Zulu* (1977). For many years, the Dillons were members of the faculty of the School of Visual Arts. They live and work in Brooklyn, New York, and have a son, Lee, who is also an artist.

SARAH DURKEE (contributing editor of *Free To Be . . . A Family*; author of "The Day Dad Made Toast," "Letters from Camp" and "The Right Family," coauthor of "Free To Be . . . A Family" "I'm Never Afraid," "It's Not My Fault," "On My Pond" and "Thank Someone") has written extensively for children's TV and theatre productions (*Sesame Street*, the Muppets, *Square One TV*); for various rock artists, including Meat Loaf and Roger Daltrey (one platinum and three gold records); and in the realm of adult (in a manner of speaking) comedy (*National Lampoon*). A native of Massachusetts, she was once forgiven for mistakenly scraping *an entire eagle* off her mother's beloved colonial wallpaper and owes "The Right Family" to that memory.

THE FAT BOYS (composer-lyricists of "Yourself Belongs to You"), one of the world's best-known rap groups, may well be the first 1000-pound trio in entertainment history. All three—Darren "The Human Beat Box" Robinson, Mark "Prince Markie Dee" Morales and Damon "Kool Rockski" Wimbley—grew up in the same East New York neighborhood, and they've been performing together since Robinson, whose family couldn't afford a drum set, perfected the technique of making percussion-like sounds with his mouth and vocal cords. Originally billed as the "Disco 3," the group changed its named soon after their manager was presented with a $350 hotel bill for "extra breakfasts." Among their credits are a platinum album, *The Fat Boys*; a Top Ten single, "Jail House Rap;" and starring roles in two motion pictures, *Krush Groove* and *Disorderlies*.

STEPHEN FLAHERTY (coauthor of "Friendly Neighborhood") is a New York-based composer and musician who writes primarily for the stage. With lyricist Lynn Ahrens, he composed the score for *The Emperor's New Clothes* and contributed musical material to *When the Cookie Crumbles . . . ,* both produced by Theatreworks/USA. In 1987, he and Ms. Ahrens won the Richard Rodgers Award for their musical *Lucky Stiff.*

JIMMY GLENN (coauthor of "Yourself Belongs to You") is the Production Manager of Tin Pan Apple Records. Since 1984, he has been the tour coordinator, confidant and co-conspirator of the Fat Boys, and during that time, he and the trio have visited over two thousand cities worldwide. He has also collaborated with the Fat Boys on the lyrics to many of their songs, and served as a Project Consultant on their movie *Disorderlies.* He and his wife Kathleen are the parents of a baby girl, Nancy Michael.

WHOOPI GOLDBERG (author of "Doris Knows Everything") is an award-winning actress, comedienne and writer. She began performing at age eight in New York with the Children's Program at the Hudson Guild and the Helena Rubenstein Children's Theater. In 1974, she moved to California, where she honed her comedy skills as a member of an improvisational group called Spontaneous Combustion. Ten years later, she wrote and starred in her own one-woman Broadway show, directed by Mike Nichols, and in 1985 she won an Oscar nomination and a Golden Globe Award for her role in Steven Spielberg's *The Color Purple.*

BOBBY GOSH (composer-lyricist of "In My Room") wrote the song "A Little Bit More," a world-wide top ten hit by Dr. Hook and the Medicine Show, which earned Mr. Gosh two gold records. He has recorded four albums of his own songs, and working in his own state-of-the-art recording studio, he has also written, produced and sung on more than two hundred national television commercials. He lives in Brookfield, Vermont, with his wife and their two children whom, he reports, were the inspiration for "In My Room."

PIERA GRANDESSO (illustrator of the music section) was born in Venice, Italy, and decided early that she wanted to be a children's book illustrator. Her dream became a reality when she was hired as a junior graphic designer and animator by a firm in Milan. Before long, her artwork was appearing regularly in a wide variety of Italian books and magazines. Ms. Grandesso moved to New York City in 1987 and now doubles as a free-lance illustrator and an animator for the Ink Tank.

CAROL HALL (contributing editor of *Free To Be . . . A Family*; composer-lyricist of "Something for Everyone") received two Drama Desk Awards for the songs she wrote for the Tony-award winning *The Best Little Whorehouse in Texas.* Ms. Hall appeared in the Broadway production of *Whorehouse,* and also starred in the hit Off-Broadway musical *I'm Getting My Act Together and Taking It on the Road.* She wrote the book, music and lyrics for the 1985 musical *To Whom It May Concern,* directed by Geraldine Fitzgerald, and her songs have been performed by such artists as Barbra Streisand, Harry Belafonte, Dolly Parton, Tony Bennett and Big Bird. Ms. Hall wrote three of the most popular songs in *Free To Be . . . You and Me*—"It's All Right To Cry," "Parents are People," and "Glad To Have a Friend Like You." A native of Abilene, Texas, Ms. Hall is married and has a grown son and daughter.

DON HAYNIE (author of "The Biggest Problem (Is in Other People's Minds)") is a songwriter, guitarist and folksinger who has been playing and singing all over North America for the past twenty years. Since 1980, he's performed with his partner, vocalist and percussionist Sheryl Samuel, and has done most of his travelling with her and their son, Seth. The duo released their first album, *Life In the Circus,* in 1986. Despite a childhood bout with polio that left him with "some of the usual after-effects," Mr. Haynie reports that he's always "had a positive attitude about finding and testing my limits, and determined for myself what I would or would not do."

CARMINE INFANTINO (illustrator of "And Superboy Makes 3") has played a pivotal role in the creation of *Superman* stories and art for more than thirty years. He came to DC Comics as a young artist in the 1950s and went on to become Editorial Director and later Publisher of the company. He is credited, in large degree, with designing the "look" comic books have today and was a pioneer in giving artists, for the first time, a strong voice in comic book production. He is now retired from full-time association with DC, but still comes back to illustrate when a project—such as "And Superboy Makes 3"—strikes his fancy.

PAUL JACOBS (composer of "Free To Be . . . A Family" and "Thank Some-one," creator of the musical arrangements for this book) has a musical background that began with Julliard training and Carnegie Hall piano debut at age nine. He was the composer and musical director of the

long-running *National Lampoon* revue, *Lemmings,* and was at one time a keyboardist and producer for the popular recording artist, Meat Loaf. He has received two ASCAP theater awards and two Grammy nominations, and the rock songs he has written have earned him several gold and platinum records.

SUSAN JEFFERS (illustrator of "Free To Be . . . A Family") is a painter and graphic artist whose exquisite illustrations for such classics as *Cinderella, Hansel and Gretel, The Wild Swans* and *Black Beauty* have earned her international recognition. She won the Caldecott Honor in 1975 for *The Three Jovial Huntsmen,* and has received literally dozens of awards and citations from such organizations as the Society of Illustrators, the International Reading Association, the Children's Book Council, the Child Study Association, the American Institute of Graphic Arts and the Biennale of Illustrations in Bratislava. Born in Oakland, New Jersey, Ms. Jeffers has worked as a book designer in three major New York publishing firms and, in collaboration with the noted author-illustrator Rosemary Wells, founded a successful art and design studio. Her family includes her husband, two adopted daughters, two stepchildren, one German shepherd and one foster kitty.

LONNI SUE JOHNSON (illustrator of "Friendly Neighborhood"), whose work is often seen in *The New Yorker, Gourmet* and many other national periodicals, is also the illustrator of the book *57 Reasons Not to Have a Nuclear War.* Artistic talent runs deep in her family—her mother and her grandmother were both also professional artists, and her husband is a composer. Illustrations by Ms. Johnson have been selected for special recognition by Graphis and by the Society of Illustrators.

MAVIS JUKES (author of "Cross Your Fingers" and "Two Can Play the Same Game") studied law at the University of California at Berkeley and was admitted to the California Bar before abandoning the legal profession to become one of America's most respected children's writers. She won a Newbery Honor in 1985 for *Like Jake and Me,* and the Irma Simonton Black Award for *No One Is Going To Nashville.* She is also the author of *Blackberries in the Dark, Lights Around the Palm* and *Getting Even.* She lives with her husband, the painter and sculptor Robert Hudson, on a farm in Northern California. Ms. Jukes has two daughters and two adult stepsons.

KERMIT THE FROG (author of "On My Pond") was born in a swamp on the outskirts of Greensboro, Mississippi, and spent most of his early years training for a career in biological laboratory work. The lure of the entertainment world soon proved too strong to resist, however, and Kermit became an instant celebrity, with starring roles in *Sesame Street, The Muppet Show* and three Muppet motion pictures, and his very own balloon in the annual Macy's Thanksgiving Day parade. Stardom hasn't spoiled him, however, and he is quick to share credit for his success with Muppet creator Jim Henson. "Every leap I've made," he says modestly, "Jim has had a hand in."

EMILY KINGSLEY (author of "Like Me") is the coauthor of *Kids Like These,* a network television movie based on her family's life. The mother of a son with Down Syndrome, she has made hundreds of lecture and media appearances to improve public attitudes about the mentally and physically disabled. She serves on the Board of Directors of the National Down Syndrome Congress, the Parent Assistance Committee for Down Syndrome and the National Media Council on Disability. Ms. Kingsley has won three Emmy Awards for her writing on *Sesame Street.* She lives with her husband, Charles, and her son, Jason, in Chappaqua, New York, and has two married stepsons.

HILARY KNIGHT (illustrator of "I'm Never Afraid") is best-known for his drawings in the juvenile (and adult) classic *Eloise,* written by Kay Thompson, which has been a best-seller for over thirty years. He has also been widely honored for the more than fifty other children's books he has illustrated, including *The Christmas Nutshell Library, The Twelve Days of Christmas* and Edward Lear's *The Owl and the Pussycat,* and for the posters he has designed for the Broadway stage. Mr. Knight was born in Roslyn, Long Island. His father, Clayton Knight, was a noted aviation artist, and his mother, Katherine Sturges, was a well-known painter, illustrator and fabric designer.

KRIS KRISTOFFERSON (coauthor of "From Here to Forever") is a member of the Country Music Songwriter's Hall of Fame, an acclaimed actor who has starred in over twenty films, a recording artist with five gold albums to his credit and a concert performer who has toured almost constantly for the better part of two decades. Born in Brownsville, Texas, Kristofferson was a college football star who graduated Phi Beta Kappa, a Golden Gloves boxer, a Rhodes Scholar, an Army helicopter pilot and a prize-winning short-story writer before turning down an offer to teach

English literature at West Point in order to pursue a career in country music. Among his best-loved compositions are "Me and Bobby McGee," "Help Me Make It Through the Night" and the 1970 Country Music Song of the Year, "Sunday Morning Coming Down." "From Here To Forever" was originally written as a lullaby for Casey, his daughter by his second wife, Rita Coolidge. He has five other children: Tracy, Jesse, Jody, John and Kris, Jr.

PIERRE LE-TAN (illustrator of "Two Can Play the Same Game") is a novelist, humorist and illustrator whose work appears frequently in *The New Yorker* and *The New York Times Magazine*. Mr. Le-Tan, who sold his first cover illustration to *The New Yorker* when he was seventeen years old, is the son of the noted Vietnamese artist Le Pho. He and his wife, Plum, live in Paris with their son and their two daughters. The Le-Tan family travel frequently together, and Mr. Le-Tan recounts their experiences on an on-going basis in *Traveller* magazine.

ARNIE LEVIN (illustrator of "The Kingdom with No Rules, No Laws, and No King" and "Letters from Camp") has been an award-winning designer, animator and cartoonist for over twenty years. He is perhaps best-known for the many covers and cartoons he has drawn for *The New Yorker*. He and his wife, Pamela, who is also a professional artist, live in Sea Cliff, New York, with their daughter, Megan, one dog and two cats.

ARNOLD LOBEL (illustrator of "I'll Fix Anthony") is one of America's best-known and best-loved children's illustrators. His sensitive and delightful drawings have appeared in more than seventy books, many of which he also wrote. Mr. Lobel won a Caldecott Honor in 1971 for *Frog and Toad Are Friends*, a Newbery Honor for its sequel *Frog and Toad Together* and the 1981 Caldecott medal for *Fables*.

PETRA MATHERS (illustrator of "A Father Like That" and "In My Room") was chosen by *The New York Times* as one of the ten best children's illustrators of 1986. Her evocative artwork has earned her two Parents Choice Awards, for the book *Maria Theresa* (which she also wrote) in 1985, and for *Molly's New Washing Machine* in 1986. She was also a finalist for the 1986 Ezra Jack Keats Award. Ms. Mathers was born in the Black Forest, in Germany, and now lives in Providence, Rhode Island, with her husband, Michael, a photographer. They have a grown son, Till.

JAMES McMULLAN (illustrator of "Thank Someone") has painted and taught illustration in New York City for more than a quarter of a century. He has won numerous Gold and Silver Medals from the Society of Illustrators and was one of five artists whose work was featured in the "Masters of the Contemporary American Poster" exhibit sponsored in 1987 by the Lowell Gallery in New York City. The child illustrated in "Thank Someone" is Mr. McMullan's daughter, Leah.

RICHARD McNEEL (illustrator of "The Day Dad Made Toast") has earned an international reputation for his unique "three-dimensional" illustrations. Among the many publications which have featured his work are *Money* magazine, *Working Mother* magazine, *Frankfurter Allgemeine Magazin*, *New Age* magazine and *Dun's Business Monthly*. An associate of the Push Pin Group, Mr. McNeel lives with his wife, Marcia, and their young daughter, Rosie. in Clifton, New Jersey.

MIRIAM MINKOWITZ (author of "A Tale of Three Ralphs") is an author, poet, philosopher and high school teacher in Brooklyn. Her stories for children have appeared in *Ms. Magazine*. Ms. Minkowitz has a doctorate in Philosophy of Education and is the mother of three grown daughters, none of whom are named Ralph.

JEFF MOSS (author of "The Entertainer") wrote the music and lyrics for *The Muppets Take Manhattan*, for which he received an Academy Award nomination. His work for the stage includes the musical *Double Feature*, directed by Mike Nichols and choreographed by Tommy Tune, and "In the Beginning," choreographed by Twyla Tharp and presented by her company at the Tyrone Guthrie Theater in Minneapolis. Mr. Moss was one of the original creators of *Sesame Street*. While serving as head writer and composer-lyricist for the program, he won five Emmy Awards and wrote songs for four Grammy Award-winning records.

JOE ORLANDO (editor of "And Superboy Makes 3") is Vice President and Creative Director of DC Comics, publishers of *Superman*, *Batman* and *Wonder Woman*. A native of Bari, Italy, whose family moved to New York when he was two years old, Mr. Orlando is also a cartoonist and illustrator whose work has been well-known over the years to readers of *Mad* magazine, *National Lampoon* and many other national periodicals. One of the highlights of his career came when *Newsweek* magazine commissioned him to draw a cover of Henry Kissinger as "Super K." Mr. Orlando and

his wife, Karin, live in Mahopac, New York, with their son and their two daughters.

ORLANDO PEREZ (author of "Twanna and Me") was born in Puerto Rico and is now a contractor in Brooklyn. He learned to read as an adult with the help of Literacy Volunteers and his eight-year-old stepdaughter, Twanna. His contribution to this book is his first published piece.

MARTHA PERSKE (illustrator of "Like Me" and "Talk It Over") launched her professional career in 1971 by illustrating her husband Robert Perske's book, *New Directions for Parents of Persons Who Are Retarded*, and since then has earned a national reputation from the artwork she had produced for juvenile and adult books, college texts, posters and advertisements. Although she does not confine her talents to drawing persons with disabilities, the remarkable beauty and sensitivity of her work has led to commissions to illustrate major reports to Presidents Nixon and Carter on mental retardation and to design the International Year of Disabled Persons commemorative stamp. Ms. Perske won the One to One Media Award in 1979, the National Association for Retarded Citizens' "ARC of Excellence Award" in 1982 and the Down Syndrome Meritorious Award in 1983.

JERRY PINKNEY (illustrator of "We and They") lives in New York City with his wife, Gloria Jean (who is also his assistant), their three sons and their daughter. A frequent contributor to *National Geographic*, he has illustrated numerous children's books and has also designed eleven stamps for the U.S. Postal Service, including the "Help in Hunger" stamp, the stamps in the Black Heritage Series and a stamp commemorating the United Way. Mr. Pinkney has twice been the recipient of the Coretta Scott King Award and has also won the Christopher Award for "artistic excellence in affirming the human spirit."

LETTY COTTIN POGREBIN (consulting editor of *Free To Be . . . A Family*; author of "A Note to Parents, Teachers, and other Grown-Up Friends" and "My Grandma") is a founding editor of *Ms. Magazine* and a founder of the Ms. Foundation. She is author of six books, including *Growing Up Free*, *Family Politics* and *Among Friends*, and she also writes and lectures nationally on children and family issues. She has won honors from such organizations as the National Council on Family Relations and the Family Service Association, and her work is featured in many textbooks and anthologies, among them *Marriage and Family*, *Beyond Sex Roles*, *Adolescent Life Experiences* and *Sexism and Youth*. Ms. Pogrebin and her husband, Bert, have three grown children— twin daughters and a son.

RALPH REESE (illustrator of "Another Cinderella") is a veteran cartoonist and illustrator whose credits include *The National Lampoon*, several national advertising campaigns and drawings for juvenile and adult books ranging from the *Choose Your Own Adventure* series, published by Bantam Books, to *The Pentagon Catalog* by Henry Beard and Christopher Cerf. He lives in Brooklyn, New York, with his wife, Barbara, a designer, who modelled for the pumpkin in Mr. Reese's "Another Cinderella" illustrations.

JACQUELINE ROGERS (illustrator of "The Right Family") has written and illustrated many successful books for children and "young adults," most of them published by Bradbury Press and Grosset & Dunlap. A graduate of the Rhode Island School of Design, Ms. Rogers likes to use relatives and close friends as models, because she feels doing so "adds warmth" to her illustrations. Her work on "The Right Family" was definitely a family affair: her two nieces, her cousin and her cousin's baby daughter all posed for her drawings.

ARTIE RUIZ (illustrator of "Jimmy Says") has designed and illustrated book covers for a wide range of publishers, including Signet, Bantam, Macmillan and Random House. He and his wife, Lisa, who is also an artist, live in Bloomfield, New Jersey. Mr. Ruiz used his cousins and his brother-in-law as models for the drawings he created for "Jimmy Says."

MARK SALTZMAN (author of "And Superboy Makes 3") writes both songs and scripts for *Reading Rainbow*, *Sesame Street* and *Square One TV*; among the stars who have performed his material are Patti Labelle, Wynton Marsalis and Itzhak Perlman. He won an Emmy Award in 1986 for his work on *Sesame Street*. He has served as a ghostwriter for the Man of Steel before, most recently as the author of *The Super-Heroes Super Healthy Cookbook*.

STACEY SCHUETT (illustrator of "From Here To Forever") lives and paints in what used to be the egg-processing plant of a chicken ranch in Petaluma, California. A native of Elmhurst, Illinois, she graduated from the University of California at Davis, where she studied art. Her work is frequently on display in Northern California galleries. Ms. Schuett's paintings for Mavis Jukes' 1987 book, *Lights Around the Palm*, resulted in her first one-person art exhibit, at Bluxon's Gallery in San Francisco.

SHEL SILVERSTEIN (author and illustrator of "Crowded Tub," "Little Abigail and the Beautiful Pony" and "The Little Boy and The Old Man") has written and illustrated several best-selling children's classics, including *Where the Sidewalk Ends, A Light in the Attic* and *The Giving Tree.* He is also a noted cartoonist and playwright and has written numerous hit songs, including "Sylvia's Mother" and "A Boy Named Sue." His story, "Ladies First," appeared in the *Free To Be . . . You and Me* book, record and television show.

CARLY SIMON (cowriter of "Turn of the Tide" and "Talk It Over") is an internationally known songwriter and performer. She won a Grammy Award for being the best new recording artist of 1971 and another in 1972 for her song "You're So Vain." Many of her songs have reached number one on the charts, and her 1987 album, *Coming Around Again*, has been a major best-seller. She is the mother of a teen-aged daughter, Sally, and a son, Ben. Ms. Simon and her colleague, Jacob Brackman, got the idea for the teacher's "freaking out" in "Talk It Over" from their friend, Mariah Garnett, who is seven.

DEBRA SOLOMON (illustrator of "Some Things Don't Make Any Sense at All" and "A Tale of Three Ralphs") is a cartoonist whose work has appeared in a wide variety of publications, from *Vogue* magazine to *The Anti-Apartheid Calendar*. She is also the illustrator of the book, *A Good Friend*, by Joseph Cohen. A native of Boston, Massachusetts, she is a graduate of Boston University and of Pratt Institute. Ms. Solomon is the president and chief operating officer of her own illustration and character-design firm, Funny Little People.

GLORIA STEINEM ("What Buying This Book Will Do") is one of America's most widely read and critically acclaimed writers and editors. Two of her books, *Outrageous Acts and Everyday Rebellions* and *Marilyn: Norma Jeane*, have been major best-sellers. Also internationally known as a feminist organizer and as a spokesperson on issues of equality, Ms. Steinem has appeared nine times on the *World Almanac*'s list of the 25 Most Influential Women in America. She is a founder of *Ms. Magazine*, the Ms. Foundation for Women, and the National Women's Political Caucus and also helped start *New York* magazine, for whom she was political columnist until 1972. She has been a recipient of the Front Page Award, the Clarion Award and the Ceres Medal from the United Nations.

JOHN STEPTOE (author-illustrator of "Stevie," illustrator of "All Us Come Cross the Water" and "The Turn of the Tide") is well-known for his groundbreaking picture books, including *Uptown, Train Ride* and *Birthday*, each of which he wrote and illustrated. Mr. Steptoe created *Stevie* when he was still a teenager. Published in 1969 by Harper & Row, it was chosen as an American Library Association Notable Book and won the Society of Illustrators' Gold Medal in 1970. Mr. Steptoe has also won a Caldecott Honor, for *The Story of Jumping Mouse*, and received The Boston Globe Horn Book Award for his 1987 book, *Mufaro's Beautiful Daughters*, published by Lothrop, Lee and Shepherd.

NORMAN STILES (contributing editor of *Free To Be . . . A Family*; author of "Another Cinderella" and "The Kingdom with No Rules, No Laws, and No King," and coauthor of "We Need a Bigger Turkey") quit his job as a supervisor in the New York City Welfare Department to become a comedy writer. Among his credits are *The Merv Griffin Show, Fernwood Tonight, America Tonight* and *The Bad News Bears*. With Mel Brooks, Mr. Stiles co-created the television series *When Things Were Rotten*, and he has also authored several successful children's books. Since 1980, he has been head writer of *Sesame Street*.

SUSAN STILLMAN (illustrator of "My Grandma") teaches illustration at the Parsons School of Design. Her work has been published in such periodicals as *The New York Times, New York* magazine, *Communications Arts* and *Scholastic* and has also appeared in several Society of Illustrators and Art Direction annuals. Ms. Stillman lives in New York with her husband, landscape architect David DeLucia, and her paintings are frequently on exhibit in galleries around the city.

PETER STONE (author of "Boy Meets Girl Plus One") is the President of the Dramatists Guild. His wide range of distinguished writing has won him an Academy Award (for *Father Goose*), an Emmy (for an episode of *The Defenders*), a Tony, a Drama Critics Circle Award and a Drama Desk Award (for *1776*), another Tony (for *Woman of the Year*) and a Mystery Writers of America Award (for *Charade*). With Carl Reiner, Mr. Stone was

the coauthor of "Boy Meets Girl," which Mel Brooks and Marlo Thomas performed on the *Free To Be . . . You and Me* record album and television special.

BILLY SWAN (coauthor of "From Here to Forever") is a composer, lyricist, guitarist and country singer with several hit songs and records to his credit. A native of Cape Girardeau, Missouri, he moved to Nashville to try to make it in the music business and ended up replacing Kris Kristofferson as night janitor for Columbia Studios after Kristofferson began to earn enough money from his own songwriting to relinquish the job. Swan and Kristofferson have been friends and colleagues ever since; Swan is often the opening act for Kristofferson's road show, and the two have collaborated on several albums. Billy Swan is married and has two children.

SIMMS TABACK (illustrator of "The Biggest Problem") has been a well-known and highly respected illustrator of children's books for over twenty years. He has received more than 100 awards from such organizations as the American Institute of Graphic Arts, the Art Directors Club of New York and the Society of Illustrators, and was included by *The New York Times* on their list of the best illustrators of juvenile books. Mr. Taback helped found both the Illustrators' Guild and the Graphic Artists Guild. He has three children and one grandchild.

MARLO THOMAS (executive editor of *Free To Be . . . A Family*; author of Foreword) is an actress, producer, and activist. She has won four Emmy awards and the prestigious George Foster Peabody Broadcasting Award. As a member of two presidential commissions on women and children, she has created a synthesis between the world of entertainment and social concern. Ms. Thomas is married to talk show host Phil Donahue.

JUDITH VIORST (author of "Some Things Don't Make Any Sense At All" and "I'll Fix Anthony!") has written twenty-two and a half books of poetry and prose for both children and adults, and is a contributing editor of *Redbook* magazine. Among her best known books are *When Did I Stop Being Twenty and Other Injustices, How To Be Hip Over Thirty* and the 1987 national bestseller, *Necessary Losses*. Ms. Viorst lives in Washington, D.C., with her husband, Milton Viorst, the political writer. They have three sons—Anthony, Nicholas, and Alexander. Ms. Viorst's story, "The Southpaw," appeared in *Free To Be . . . You and Me*.

KURT VONNEGUT, JR. (author of the Afterword) is the best-selling author of many novels, including *Slaughterhouse Five, Cat's Cradle, Player Piano, The Sirens of Titan* and *Blue Beard*. He was born in Indianapolis, Indiana, and now lives and works in Manhattan. Mr. Vonnegut, who is married to the photographer and author Jill Krementz, was inducted into the National Institute of Arts and Letters in 1970. He also contributed an Afterword to *Free To Be . . . You and Me*.

JANE WAGNER (author of ". . . But First This Message") has received four Emmys for her work in television and a George Foster Peabody Award for her teleplay *I.T.* She also wrote the screenplay for *The Incredible Shrinking Woman*. She has received three Grammy nominations, and on Broadway she wrote and directed the Tony Award-winning *Appearing Nightly*. Most recently, she received the New York Drama Desk and New York Drama Critics Circle Awards for her work as writer-director of the play *The Search for Signs of Intelligent Life in the Universe*, starring Lily Tomlin, which has also been a major best-selling book.

GARY ZAMCHICK (illustrator of "Doris Knows Everything," "It's Not My Fault" and "The Stupid Song") is well known for his witty cartoons as well as his elaborate computer graphics. His work appears weekly in the Arts & Leisure section of *The New York Times*. Mr. Zamchick has worked at Push Pin Studios and also spent two years at Time, Inc. designing children's educational software. He is now the president of his own graphics firm, DadaBase Design.

CHARLOTTE ZOLOTOW ("A Father Like That") is one of America's most distinguished authors and editors. She is the author of over sixty books that portray the everyday experiences of young children and their discovery of the world around them and is the editor-in-chief of a line of juvenile books published under her own imprint. Ms. Zolotow is the recipient of numerous awards, including the Harper Gold Medal Award for Editorial Excellence and several American Library Association citations. Her story "William's Doll," for which she received a *Redbook* magazine Award, appeared in *Free To Be . . . You and Me*. A native of Norfolk, Virginia, she is the mother of two children, including the nationally-known children's author, Crescent Dragonwagon.